So Over You

You

GWEN HAYES

ISBN:1492981672
ISBN-13: 978-1492981671

OTHER BOOKS BY GWEN HAYES

Falling Under
Dreaming Awake
Ours is Just a Little Sorrow
Totally Tubular

CONTENTS

1 CHAPTER ONE

EVEN though I'd already blown right past the "do not exceed" warning on my Excedrin bottle, I popped two more without water and surveyed the scene before me.

A sorrier crew of journalists would be hard to find. Fitting, since, technically, we no longer had a school newspaper due to district budget cuts. What we did have, besides the bunch of fools currently yelling at each other, was a classroom with three ancient computers, an unpaid advisor, six "journalists," and two co-chief editors. Yours truly and...well, I liked to call him Beelzebub.

Everyone else called him Jimmy Foster.

Our after-school staff meeting began the same way we've begun every staff meeting this year—with an argument. Only this one was pretty heated. We had a forest fire on our hands, and my co-editor seemed to be clutching a lighter instead of a fire hose.

Foster and I stared each other down from opposite ends of the thirty-year-old folding table

1

while the rest of the crew tried to get individual points of view across by raising the volume of the argument and moving their arms a lot.

The argument wasn't even relevant to the news. Nobody fought for first dibs on a hot story or argued over bylines and cover copy. No, they were upset over fundraisers. More specifically, our fundraiser.

Chaos.

I missed the days of hard-boiled reporting. We only had one returning staff member. The rest were too young, too idealistic, and far too grating on my nerves. That was probably my fault, though.

It wouldn't be an exaggeration to call me neurotic. I'm not good with people. I tend to be brisk and seemingly uncaring. I'm the girl who never got hired to babysit a second time by the same family. It seems I lack certain…skills. Namely patience.

Mr. Blake kept reminding me that I needed to be a mentor, so I kept hitting the Excedrin and praying for a break in the clouds.

Or at least a little help from my "partner."

I folded my arms across my chest and raised one arched brow. My nemesis responded by unfolding his limbs in a giant stretch and then clasped his hands behind his head as if he didn't have a care in the world. Of course, he had to do that maneuver every so often. His big fat head would cause him terrible neck strain if he didn't take frequent breaks to support the weight of it in his hands.

This was going to be a long year. I worked hard to get this position on the paper, and I wasn't pleased I had to share it with such an arrogant excuse for a reporter. I'm sure he had some good traits; I'd just never witnessed any in the years we'd worked on staff.

I checked my watch. We needed to calm down the children or Mommy and Daddy were never going to put the first issue to bed.

I stood up slowly and cleared my throat. Several times. I shot the evil genius a look that meant do something, so he put his fingers in his mouth and whistled. Everyone covered their ears and shut up; he had a way about him, that's for sure.

Foster appealed to some girls. I didn't understand the draw, but several of our staff were girls with new "aspirations" in journalism, and they hung on his every word. Blech. While it's true his evil black soul didn't show from the outside, he still wasn't the kind of guy you'd want a poster of on your wall. At least I wouldn't. Unless I drew a bull's-eye on it and used it for dart practice.

It was annoying the way the new girls pandered to his ego all the time. "Jimmy, what do you think?" "Jimmy, is this a good idea?" "Jimmy, I always get confused—is it their or there?" "Jimmy, do you think it's annoying or cute when a girl dots her "i"s with a heart?" "Jimmy, is it true you won the Aronsen Achievement Award for Excellence in Journalism last year?"

Well, okay, he did win the award. We were both finalists, but his interview with a survivor from Wesley High after a student shooting incident was exceptional. I'll give him that much.

And he could sure whistle.

Since I finally had everyone's attention, I began, "I'm not sure the calendar idea is going to work."

The whining commenced immediately, but Foster brought his fingers back to his lips and everyone shut up and covered their ears again. I fought a smirk—they had no idea how easily they were being trained. When we were freshmen, the editor used to smack our hands with a ruler. I'm not an advocate of corporal punishment, and he did serve a lot of detention over it, but our staff meetings ran a lot smoother that year. Just sayin'.

I restarted, tapping my fingers on the pseudo-wood table even though I itched for a ruler. "As a fund-raiser, the idea is original but problematic. For one thing, it's objectifying."

Foster laughed. "I'll never understand why girls wear tight clothes and short skirts and then complain that we like to look at them."

I exhaled and counted to five. "Some girls haven't learned yet that their real value isn't what part of the body they are exposing. This newspaper is not going to capitalize on their low self-esteem."

Foster stood and all heads snapped back to his end of the table. "Some girls have high enough self-esteem to realize that their appearance is an asset, not an obstacle." He scanned my outfit meaningfully, as if he found it lacking, and then grabbed both corners of the table and leaned toward me. "We need a fundraiser. We'd have to have a car wash every Saturday until May to earn the kind of revenue we could earn from making a calendar."

I copied his pose. "I won't endorse this idea just so you can ogle a new cheerleader every month."

"You jealous, Logan?"

"No, but I'm beginning to taste bile, Foster."

Like at a tennis match, the staff followed our word volley with their turning heads.

"Fine, we'll do a calendar with the football team,

then," he answered. As if that solved anything.

"So it's not objectifying if it's boys?"

"We don't care. For crying out loud, my mother has a calendar of cats in the kitchen. Do we need to call PETA? Is she objectifying felines?"

I rolled my eyes. Did Foster ever take a break from being Foster? "Why do you want to do a calendar so badly? I don't see what's in it for you."

He shrugged. "You may not see what's in it for me, but when you stand like that, I can see down your shirt."

I had to bite my tongue. There wasn't much I could do about the flush creeping across my skin and threatening to set fire to the roots of my hair, but I could control my temper. Barely.

Resisting the urge to check the status of my shirt, I unclenched my fingers from the table and eased back into my chair.

"We wouldn't have to objectify the boys," said Maryanne, one of the newer sophomore girls. "What if we wrote meaningful exposés on each player?"

Chelsea snorted. "How many meaningful things are you going to find about the football team?" Thank goodness for returning staff. I knew she wouldn't let me down. "We should do the soccer team instead. They have a broader ethnic background too. And ohmigawd, their butts are to die for."

Though gaping is unattractive, I couldn't help it. I thought for sure Chelsea would have agreed with me that the whole idea of personifying any student's physical appearance as character traits to be lauded in such in impersonal way was just wrong. I mean she was a vegan. She wore sandals and patchouli.

All the girls began arguing again, this time over

which team was the sexiest and therefore deserved a year of leering. I nibbled at the inside of my cheek and rubbed small circles into my temples as I watched Jimmy Foster make notes in his spiral notebook. An evil grin spread across his face and I narrowed my eyes. What was he up to?

He scribbled in earnest, bent over so I could only see the top of his mussed-up hair. The little gelled-up spikes were dark, but when you get him in sunlight, his hair is redder, especially at his temples. He looked up from his notebook, but I didn't avert my gaze. He'd already caught me staring at him; I wouldn't give him the satisfaction of being embarrassed by it.

A slow smile slithered across his face and he winked at me. He was plotting something horrid. There was no other explanation for his apparent happiness. Every time that boy smiled, somewhere a puppy died.

"Okay, we got it." Chelsea smiled, playing with the ends of her braid. Speaking for the group, she stood. "We want to do a photo shoot with each boy from a different school club or sport." She shot me a quelling look. "We'll have meaningful verbiage for each one and the whole project will be about diversity and un-objectifying the male species on campus."

"It's a great idea," I chirped, despite the throbbing in my temples and the churning in my gut.

Foster narrowed his eyes. "Did you just say it was a great idea?"

"Well it goes against all my principles, which means it's sure to rake in the dough. And we need a lot of it." I wanted to thrash Chelsea with her own Birkenstocks, but instead I smiled complacently.

We'd already resigned ourselves to putting out the

Follower, our newspaper, digitally only this year, but we still needed better software to pull that off. The school had given us a budget of minus one hundred dollars (they still wanted the money we went over budget last year). If that meant we had to whore out our integrity, so be it. The one thing I wouldn't do was let the paper fold. Not on my watch.

Mr. Blake, our esteemed and unpaid advisor, and the sophomore he took with him—I forget his name—returned from the coffee run. So, of course, all forward progress stalled as he called out complicated coffee orders.

"Tall half-skinny, sugar-free vanilla."

"Right here," said Maryanne.

Ugh. This was going to take a while. I pushed away from the table and found the box of freebie software we'd liberated from an old storage closet. Hopefully, there would be something compatible with the three different operating systems we had to choose from.

Another order up. "Quad shots with heavy foam and Splenda, not Sweet'N Low."

Foster pitched himself onto the table next to the box. "What is going on in that devious head of yours?"

"What do you mean?" I held up an eight-inch square. "What is this?"

"That's a floppy disk. I'd say circa 1985. And you know what I mean. You hate the calendar idea. Why'd you go along with it?"

I shrugged. "I don't have much choice. I'm outnumbered."

"Soy frappé, no whip. Who had the soy?" Mr. Blake asked.

"Chelsea," everyone answered, and Foster and I

rolled our eyes.

"It will make a lot of money, Logan. We need it."

"I know, I know." I sighed. "I bet we can get the cardstock donated if we advertise the stationery store."

"Two black coffees."

Foster and I raised our hands.

Mr. Blake joined us. "What's this about a Stud of the Month the girls are yammering about?"

"Fundraiser," I offered.

"And," Foster added, taking both coffees and handing me one. "A really great feature story."

"Feature?" Something told me I was going to hate this idea.

"Listening to all those girls argue about which guys were worthy enough to make the calendar, I couldn't help but wonder…" He looked me straight on with his devil eyes. "What is it, exactly, that girls are looking for in high school boys?"

"Are we Cosmo Teen now?" I asked. "And you sound like Carrie Bradshaw from *Sex and the City* with all that 'I couldn't help but wonder' crap. Where is the feature story in this? I don't see it."

Using his TV announcer voice, Foster began, "A year of dates in six weeks. Our intrepid girl reporter de-objectifies the calendar boys by spending time with each model and extolling the experience in an award winning exposé into the mind of a teenage female." Nerves under my skin began racing to get away. Far, far away. "Culminating, of course, with the release of the beefcake calendar."

"So you want to send one of our reporters on twelve dates with virtual strangers?"

"No, I want to send you on twelve dates. The

8

stranger part is just a bonus."

Like hell. "Me? I don't date high school boys."

There are plenty of reasons not to swim in the dating pool that is high school. But the root source of my reluctance to dive right in has always been avoidance of the questionable warm spots in the water.

It's not so much that high school boys are stupid or even immature. It's just that they're, well, high school boys.

"Which is exactly why you are the obvious choice."

"It's a terrible idea." I turned to Mr. Blake. "I'm not comfortable with this idea at all."

Mr. Blake, my hero, my mentor, the English teacher who taught me to think and the journalism teacher who taught me to think for myself, rubbed the silver whiskers on his face and betrayed me. "Sometimes a good reporter needs to challenge her comfort zone. Break out. Question her world."

Lucifer waggled his eyebrows and gloated.

"I can't believe you are taking his side," I whined.

Mr. Blake nodded toward the staff. "I suggest you get your newsroom back under control so you can hammer out some details."

It's amazing what the right motivation coupled with caffeine could do for a staff of my peers. They took the cover shoot and twelve blind date ideas and ran as if they'd been handed the Olympic torch. While I was pleased that, only two weeks into the school year, several of them were beginning to show leadership and organizational skills, I was a little miffed that nobody was even a little worried about my safety. Or sanity.

Under Foster's direction, my role in the calendar had been eliminated completely. Ordinarily, the release would have been a relief. Since I had to date these guys, though, I wished for at least veto power.

I tried to get out of the Twelve Dates of Doom; really, I did. When I realized I was scared to do it, I stopped arguing. Backing down from a challenge is so not the girl I am. Here I was fighting to save a newspaper that didn't exist; a dozen dates should be easy in comparison.

After everyone but Foster and I filed out of the room, I slumped into my seat and appraised the newsroom. For three years, this room was my magic place. The *Follower* lived and breathed here. The paper, iconic to our school and town, always forged ahead of its time and without regard to those that would stifle the truth. Sometimes controversial, always relevant, it meant something to be on staff—a mark of character and integrity.

Now the magic place festered in bureaucracy and constraints. No funding, no class time, no paid advisor. Foster and I had agreed on one thing in all the years we'd served the paper, and that was that we would do whatever it took to keep it alive this year. We'd been handed fistfuls of nothing, but we had no intention of failure. The school let us have the room but commandeered the working computers and anything else it could salvage for other classrooms. It was like starting over, only worse because we had so much to live up to.

It made a girl tired.

"Your car still in the shop?" Foster asked me.

I nodded.

"I can give you a ride."

I so didn't want a ride but resigned myself to it anyway. "Thanks."

Foster handed me the messenger bag I'd flung over my chair. "It's going to be great, you know."

"Huh?"

"The paper. This year. I can tell you're worried about it, but it's going to be great. We're going to make this work."

I wanted to believe him. "Sure."

He threw himself into my path, halting me. You think I'd be used to it, literally and figuratively. It's what he lived for—stopping me from forward progress. "Logan, you need to trust it or it won't happen."

Not for the first time since the powers that be yanked out the rug, tears formed and stung the back of my eyes. Not shedding them had become one of my personality quirks. Some people snap gum; I fight tears.

"Trust? That's a little oxymoronic for good reporters, isn't it?"

"Layney Logan, there are two things in this world you don't need to question. One is gravity." He tilted my chin to force me to look him in the eye. The sudden intimacy shocked me. "The other is Layney Logan. If you want this bad enough, you'll make it happen." He dropped his hand but didn't move away.

My stomach flipped like one of Mom's Sunday morning pancakes.

The devil was his most dangerous when he wasn't being devilish. I had to remind myself of that during the weird beat of time that stood still while we remained anchored in place and far too close to each other.

Desperate to say something to break his wicked spell, I went with exactly the wrong thing. "I really want this to happen."

He blinked. "Me too."

The dimple in his top lip drew my gaze like a swinging pendant held by a hypnotist. He swallowed and I tilted my head so that I was looking up at him through my eyelashes. Like I was...flirting?

I stepped back quickly. "Great. So we're on the same page about the paper then."

He nodded and then cleared his throat. "Yeah. We're on the exact same page. We should go."

"See? I was thinking the same exact thing."

He handed me his keys. "I'll meet you in the lot. I forgot something in my locker."

His hand brushed mine as my fingers clasped the key ring and I realized he had to be messing with me. Nothing happens naturally when you are dealing with the king of deception. Everything he's ever said or done to me was planned in advance and carried out with stealth.

Foster almost fooled me that time. I turned out the lights and closed the door behind me.

He wouldn't get a second chance.

2 CHAPTER TWO

Mr. January

TURNS out Maryanne was a stellar add to our staff. Her father owned the pawn shop on Main and Cedar, so we added two gently used computers to our inventory. Elden, the sophomore whose name I had previously forgotten and the only boy on staff (because demons don't count), and I were trying to network the computers and clean off all the porn. Poor Elden's face couldn't have gotten any redder.

Me, it didn't bother so much. I'm still trying to figure out what that says about my personality.

I sensed evil before I felt Foster crouch between our chairs. "See, Elden." Foster pointed to the naughty woman on the screen. "If Mommy wore outfits like that more often, Daddy wouldn't spend so much time at the bar."

"Yes, well, if Daddy didn't spend so much time at the bar, he'd know that Mommy wears outfits like that for the milkman every night."

Poor Elden's eyes widened even larger beneath his Coke-bottle glasses. He didn't know what to make of either of us. It's not like I sat around trying to find ways to traumatize the more innocent members of our staff, but I'll admit I found it a perk.

"Elden, it's Friday night. Go home." Foster swiped Elden's seat after the kid shot out of his chair obligingly. "You ready for your big date?" he asked.

"As ready as I intend to be."

"Is that what you're wearing?"

I looked at my cargo pants and long-sleeve tee. "What's wrong with what I'm wearing?"

Satan shrugged. "Nothing. Some guys like that look, I guess."

"And what look is that?"

He perused me slowly with his gaze. "Salvation Army meets Bohemian pixie."

I snorted. "I am none of those things." Well, okay, my jacket came from the Army Surplus store, and I am short. I don't consider myself Bohemian, though. My wardrobe lacks the creativity required to pull that off.

"You ready for you assignment?"

Ugh. No. I'd rather go undercover at cheer camp and spend a week pretending I cared what the secret to school spirit is. That's how desperately I wanted out of this assignment. "Lay it on me."

He pushed a pink note across the tabletop. I unfolded it slowly, willing my shaky fingers not to give me away. Unfolded, the "assignment" was in the shape of a heart.

Very funny.

Dessert and coffee at Mick's.
Reservation in the name of Love.
6:30.

I couldn't summon spit if my life depended on it. My mouth dried out like I'd swallowed desert sand. "Who's paying for this date, anyway?"

"The marketing department has been working very hard at soliciting corporate sponsors."

Since we didn't have a marketing department, even during the good years, I pursed my lips and waited for a better explanation.

"Misty and Rachel are getting the local businesses to donate cost of the date for the free advertising. Don't forget to mention the tiramisu at Mick's when you write up your story."

Great. Product placement. I'd already sold myself out and I wasn't even eighteen.

"Is your car running today?" Foster asked.

I hated my car. It worked three out of seven days, and the other four were sketchy. "Maybe. It wouldn't start again this morning. It might be fine now."

"You need to get rid of that piece of junk and find something reliable."

"I had to quit my after school job to get the paper off the ground and I'm not touching my college money. I can hoof it."

"I'll give you a ride."

"You're going to drop me off for a date? That's not weird or anything." I reached between us to power down the computer, careful not to brush his leg with my arm. But not careful enough, I noticed too late, to stop him from looking down the scoop neck of my shirt.

15

He picked up my cell and pushed my hand away when I tried to grab it away from him. "Just making sure you charged it."

Plucking it from him, I pocketed the phone and shot him a dirty look. "Why the sudden concern?"

"A good chief is always worried about his tribe. And before you get all pissy, yes, I know we're co-chiefs. And yes, I'm aware that I've probably gotten all your feminist hackles on red alert. Not to mention your politically correct ones. Frankly, my dear...well, you know the rest."

"So, who am I meeting tonight?"

He waggled his finger at me. "Nice try, tricky minx. You know I can't tell you that. It would be against the rules."

"Did he sign the contract?"

"Of course."

The contract was the only concession I had been allowed. It stated in no uncertain terms that:

- There would be no physical contact.
- There would be no attempts to communicate after the date unless both parties were agreeable. And then only after the calendar hit the stands.
- The date would last exactly sixty minutes and no more.
- The date would remain confidential until the story was published.
- There would be no physical contact.

(I made sure they put that condition in the contract twice to punctuate the seriousness of the clause.)

"You sure you don't want to change clothes before the date? We have time."

Did I have time to wipe that smirk off his face with a heated iron? "You're one to talk. Charlie Brown called. He wants his shirt back."

He wiped invisible dust off his shoulder. "Well, he's not getting it. The shirt looks much better on me."

Foster's clothes reminded me my grandfather's closet, and I wouldn't be surprised if some of his camp shirts were vintage '50s. Somehow, it didn't make him look as stupid as if anyone else tried to pull it off. I mean he had bowling shirts and argyle sweaters, for God's sake. Normal high-school students can't get away with dressing like Richie Cunningham.

We reviewed our notes about possible web hosts and story ideas for the next forty-five minutes. Then, with feet of lead, I followed him out to his reliable Ford Escort. The ride to Mick's was fraught with danger. I couldn't let Foster smell my fear or I'd be as good as carnage. He would zero in on any perceived weakness and exploit the soft spot until I turned into one giant bruise.

I decided he must be after my total annihilation with this whole date thing. He probably didn't want to go halves on the editor-in-chief position. If he broke me, he wouldn't have to share the job.

I sat up straighter in my seat. Too bad for him. I wasn't going anywhere. There would be a feature story in this craziness. Maybe not the story he envisioned in his plot to overtake my position, but I'd find the real one. The one that made him sorry he ever messed with Layney Logan.

"What now?" he asked.

"What do you mean?"

"You just did that thing you do whenever you think you're going to win an argument with me, only we weren't arguing."

"What thing do I do?"

"You sit up all straight and thrust your chin out. I wasn't even talking, so I don't know what you could be mad at me for."

"Gee, I don't know, Foster. Maybe this whole ridiculous dating scheme you came up with? What do you possibly have to gain?"

"What do you have to lose?" He pulled up to the curb in front of the restaurant. "God, you act like it's some kind of death sentence. I'm probably doing you a favor."

"Excuse me?"

"Going on a few dates will be good for you. Get you out in the world a little."

"I don't need you to decide what's good for me."

"I'm just saying that you shouldn't hold on to the past so much."

It's possible that the blood in my veins just came to a complete stop and then started flowing backward. "What are you trying to say?"

I knew exactly what he was trying to say.

"Never mind. It wasn't important. We're here. You should go warm up and stretch before the main event. You don't want to pull a muscle."

"What. Were. You. Trying. To. Say?"

He pinched the bridge of his nose. I wanted to hit the bridge of his nose with a cement block. "Look, it's just a little…sad…that you haven't gone out with anyone since…you know."

The roar of the ocean filled my head. "I can't believe you went there." I glared at him and then rolled my eyes. "Oh, wait. It's you. Yes, I can."

I undid my seatbelt so I could strangle him. "Do you honestly, truly, really believe that you are the reason I don't date? Of course you do. What am I thinking? That was four years ago."

"I know."

"We were in the eighth grade."

"I know. Which is why it's kind of tragic."

"I'm not having this discussion with you." Just because Foster slept with half the female population didn't mean I was less over him for not turning into a slut. "Besides, I have dated. Just not high school boys."

"Sure."

He said "sure" but he obviously didn't mean "sure." It would have been nice to wipe that patronizing look off his face. Instead, I had responsibilities to attend. "College guys are more mature than guys my own age, but that's a discussion for a different day. Right now, I have an interview to go to."

"It's a date."

"It's an interview."

"Whatever. I'll pick you up in an hour." He sat there looking smug. His broad smile, his relaxed pose—I wanted to kill him. And then revive him so I could kill him again.

"Don't bother." I slammed the door shut, closing my jacket in. I couldn't tug it out, so I had to open the door again. "I mean it; don't bother."

"Toodles." He waved and pulled away after I slammed the door again.

My phone vibrated in my pocket. I looked at the caller I.D:

Prince of Darkness

"What?" I barked.

"Don't forget you aren't allowed to record the date."

"It's an interview, and if he gives me permission, I can."

"No, you can't. No notes either. You can doodle all you want after, but during the date, you have to act like a girl."

Needless to say, I ended the call.

Act like a girl. He set me up so I'd be as flustered as possible. He wanted me to fail. Otherwise why would he have brought up eighth grade? As far as I'm concerned, eighth grade never happened.

I marched into Mick's and stopped at the hostess desk.

"Good evening. How may I help you?"

My heart sank. The hostess was one of those women who make you feel uncultured and immature just by looking at her. Her makeup was flawless, her hair sleek and shiny, and somehow even her black skirt and white blouse looked high fashion.

I cleared my throat. "I have reservations at 6:30 in the name of...Love." I tried to force a smile through clenched teeth. Name of Love. Seriously, who could blame me for wanting to send Jimmy Foster through a meat grinder at this point?

She smiled sweetly. "Of course you do. Right this way. Your party has already arrived."

Great. I'd been hoping for a few minutes to pull myself together.

Mick's is not a place most high schoolers go unless

it's their mother's birthday or out-of-town relatives are visiting. Not that it isn't nice; there's just something about jazz and white tablecloths that make you feel like you're twelve again. I clutched my messenger bag tightly in case it knocked over a water glass or candle.

She led me to a corner, thank God, and waited expectantly for my date to stand. Only he didn't know that's what she was waiting for. The uncomfortable twelve seconds passed more like ten minutes worth of painful silence. She finally realized neither of us knew what we were doing and pointed to my chair. "Enjoy your dinner."

My mind tried to process the small details of my date's face while I struggled to place him. I'd seen him before, but I didn't know who he was. My biggest fear was that Foster would set me up with twelve trolls. This guy was actually cute. He had a little unfortunate acne, but nothing was glaringly hideous. Sandy brown hair, blue eyes, and he'd worn a nice sweater.

So far so good.

"Hi, I'm Layney."

"I'm Chuck."

When he didn't follow that statement with anything, I realized I was going to have to use my interviewing skills after all. Open-ended questions were going to be my friends. If I relied on yes-or-no answers, we would never get anywhere.

I worked up my cheery smile. "I'm sort of nervous. I've never been on a blind date before. Have you?"

"No."

See what I mean about yes-or-no questions?

Take two. "So what made you decide to do this?"

He shrugged.

Our waiter brought over the dessert menu and coffee. I ordered the tiramisu just in case that really was part of the conditions for the owner picking up the tab.

"Chuck, do you play any sports?"

"Basketball."

That's where I'd seen him. "What made you choose basketball over, say, baseball?"

He smiled. "I'm six-four." And then he blushed.

Shyness I can empathize with. While I wasn't much on dating, it wasn't because I was shy. Shyness doesn't get great stories. I tended to be a little more…aggressive. But I also knew how to set people at ease, make them comfortable enough to spill their guts to me.

Well, okay, sometimes I made people uncomfortable. Just not usually the ones I interviewed.

I broke the elbows-on-the-table rule and rested my chin in my hands. "Okay, let's get this out right now, then. You're tall, handsome, and a varsity ball player. And you are obviously not the kind of guy that goes out of his way to get into calendars. Why are you on a blind date with me?" I even batted my eyelashes.

He started to say something, but our food arrived. One tentative bite later and I was hooked on tiramisu. "Oh my God, this is good. Is yours good?"

He nodded. "It's vanilla ice cream. But yeah, it tastes good." And then he pushed it away. "God, I'm so stupid."

"What's wrong?"

He covered his face in his hands. I checked out the room to make sure nobody was staring at us. If he started crying, I was going to have to take a vow of agoraphobia and spend the rest of my life in my room.

"Chuck?"

He moved his hands out of the way—fortunately, no tears. "I'm sorry. I just feel so stupid. I mean, no wonder she broke up with me."

"I'm going to need a map or something, Chuck. I'm not following you at all." *Please don't cry. Please don't cry.* Foster would never let it die if I made a boy cry on my first date.

He exhaled and went back to his ice cream. "I'm boring. I can never think of the right things to say, and I order vanilla ice cream, and everything about me is uninteresting."

Okay, then. Boys got insecure too, I could see. "Your three-pointers are pretty amazing," I offered.

"That's the problem. My girlfriend, she thinks—well, she thought—that basketball is all I care about. And it's not. It's just the only thing I know I'm good at. She broke up with me, but she doesn't understand."

"What doesn't she understand?"

"She's all I think about. Not basketball. Not sports. That's why I agreed to do this. I thought maybe she'd get jealous. But that's probably dumb too."

If that wasn't the sweetest thing ever, I don't know what is. She was obviously a moron. "Here's the thing. I'm totally lame at the whole relationship thing because, well, I choose not to have them; but did you ever tell your *girlfriend* what you just told me?"

He shook his head. "Can I try your…whatever that is?"

I pushed my plate to him. I wasn't going to stand in someone's way while they tried to break out of their comfort zone.

"This isn't bad."

"Vanilla ice cream is good too, though, Chuck. Tell me about your girlfriend."

Chuck smiled. "She's amazing. She's so smart and really pretty. She went to every single home game last year, even when she was sick. God, she was so supportive of me, but I totally blew it. I never even tried to learn about the stuff she liked. I just assumed she was happy doing the stuff I liked."

When he finally took a breath, I asked him if she was still available.

"Yeah. I think so."

"Then promise me you'll try to get her back, Chuck."

"You don't think it's too late?"

A girl like me had no business giving relationship advice. The only real boyfriend I'd had turned into hellfire's answer to John Mayer after we broke up, but I liked Chuck and really wanted him to be happy. "Just because you took too much for granted before, doesn't mean you can't learn from your mistakes. Tell her you're sorry, that she was the best thing that ever happened to you, and that you wished you had appreciated her more when you were together. Then tell her all the mushy stuff about how you feel."

"Mushy stuff."

"Yeah, you know," I mumbled while sweeping my hands in the air. "Like, she's the only thing you think about, you're so in love, yada yada yada."

"Yada yada yada?"

"Oh, don't actually say that part. Some people get

24

touchy about stuff like that."

He crinkled his brow. "Are you sure you're a girl?"

I shrugged. "Most of the time." Just not your average girl. Hearts and flowery talk gave me hives.

By the time our date ended, I'd helped Chuck write out a script for making up with his girlfriend. We even had Plan B and Plan C, depending on how well she responded—or how well she didn't. He told me over and over how this was the best date he'd ever been on. I told him he probably shouldn't share that little nugget with his ex.

We stood in front of the restaurant, and I broke the rules and hugged him goodbye.

My ride home was less than amused.

"That was irresponsible and unethical, Logan."

"What is your problem?" I'd barely buckled myself in before Foster peeled out into the street.

"A good reporter knows the boundaries of an interview."

"I thought it was a date."

His white knuckles looked stark against the black of the steering wheel. "There were signed contracts. I can't believe you just…"

"Just what? Acted like a girl?"

Foster didn't say another word to me until he pulled into my driveway. "How was the tiramisu?"

I slid out of my seat. "It was better than I expected."

3 CHAPTER THREE

Mr. February

MONDAY morning found me where every weekday morning found me—in the newsroom before school trying to figure out what I'd done to deserve the mess I'd been handed. Someone had dumped several cases of old textbooks in the middle of our newsroom before I'd gotten there that morning. I guessed we were now the new school storage closet. As I lugged them to the corner and stacked them against a wall, I tried to sort out some of my to-do list.

We still needed to recruit a decent photographer, especially for the calendar. We also still needed to come up with some regular columns and find some investigative stories to report on. Plus we needed to learn web design because not one of those new girls knew any code at all, and I sure as heck didn't.

Only a few weeks ago, I'd been blissfully unaware of the jam I'd be in. I looked forward to my senior year. Until Mr. Blake called Foster and me to the school a week before class started.

"As you know, the school district—our entire community—is facing some tough economic choices," Mr. Blake had begun. "There's no easy way to say this, kids—they've cut journalism from the schedule. The local newspaper is shutting down too, which means there will be no *Follower* this year."

It was the day the music died for me. And not the Madonna version either, thanks.

The local paper used to do our print runs for free. With them out of business, we couldn't go to print, which is why we opted for a web version. Why we opted for any version at all had more to do with pride and stubbornness. The two things Foster and I had in common.

Trying to resurrect the institution that once was the paper consumed me. So much so that I didn't realize I was no longer alone in the newsroom until someone cleared her throat.

"How was your date?" Maryanne asked. Right away, my Spidey sense tingled. Typically, Maryanne was not one of the before-school visitors. Sometimes she came in at lunch, but usually just after school. She was also the only girl who wasn't always hanging all over Foster.

"It wasn't bad," I answered. "He was pretty nice." I watched her body language closely.

Maryanne didn't look at me, instead traced her finger back and forth across the scarred tabletop. "Did you think he was…interesting?"

"I suppose so. He was kind of…" I was about to say vanilla when I realized she was working extra hard at acting nonchalant. "Obsessed."

She nodded and sighed. "With sports, right?" She twisted her ring, "I mean, you know, like all boys."

"No. In fact, he barely talked about basketball at all."

Her head shot up, and her eyes blazed with curiosity. "What was he obsessed with, then?"

I shrugged and powered up a computer. "His ex-girlfriend."

One. Two. Three.

"Really?"

"Yeah. He had zero interest in dating me at all. Or anyone else. I think he just went along with the idea to find out what girls are looking for. I think he'd do anything to get her back." Even date me.

"Really? Huh." She bit her lip. "So what did he say about his girlfriend?"

"You mean his ex-girlfriend."

"Yeah."

"Maryanne…why don't you ask him yourself?"

Her cheeks pinkened. "What do you mean?"

"Never try to hide your motives from a reporter. We can smell deception like garlic. Chuck is still crazy about you."

"I don't know what you're talking about." But her smile said differently.

"He even tried tiramisu last night."

"What is tiramisu?" she asked.

"Exactly."

I love it when people have little light bulb moments. I only had to wait a second before she realized that I was telling her that her boyfriend was at least trying to overcome his inclination toward all things boring.

"Maryanne, the paper still needs a sportswriter. I

think you should sign up for that position."

"But I don't know much about sports, except maybe basketball."

"It's a shame. None of us on staff do, really. Elden and Foster aren't exactly fanatics either."

"His name is Alden."

"Huh?"

"The guy you keep calling Elden is really Alden."

"Oh. Wow. He must hate me."

"No more than he hates Jimmy," she agreed.

"Meh. Everybody should hate Foster. Anyway, it's too bad that nobody here knows very much about sports. Even if someone wanted to learn more about them, that would be helpful. Like, if they knew somebody who could spend time teaching them about sports or something."

She crossed her arms. "You think I should have Chuck help me write the sports stories, don't you?"

"I might be thinking that he knows too much about sports and not enough about you—and you know all about you but nothing about sports."

"I'll, um, think about it."

"You do that."

After Maryanne left, I had one blissful moment of solitude before Lucifer joined me.

I hopped on the table. "Hey, Satan, how's it going?" I asked.

"Fantastic. I recommend beginning every day bathing in the blood of sacrificed virgins. It's quite invigorating. How was your weekend? Did you clip coupons and knit socks for the war effort?" He stood in front of me and dropped his books on the table to my right.

"No, sadly, my sciatica was acting up again. Hey,

29

did you know Elden's name is Alden?"

"Who is Elden?"

"Never mind. What do you think of Maryanne taking the sports section with help from her jock boyfriend?"

"Can he write?"

"I have no idea. But he can translate the stats into English."

"That might have to be enough. It's more than we have right now, anyway. Maybe they can do a 'He Said/She Said' column."

"Nice." I scribbled down a note on his spiral notebook with the pen he'd left on top of it "Don't let me forget to pitch that idea to her this afternoon. What's on our agenda this week?"

"I need to start booking photo shoots with the super models until we get a new photographer. Sounds like you may have wrapped up our sports section. We still need to figure out the website design or we'll end up using a free blog."

"That's not a bad idea. Unless we can recruit someone from the computer tech classes, that would be cooler. When is my next calendar interview?"

"Your next date is Wednesday. Maybe you should get a haircut or something."

"What is wrong with my hair?" I held up my hand. "No, don't tell me. I don't care."

"That's sort of what's wrong with your hair."

Even though it meant showing weakness, I couldn't help patting my ponytail. I was low-maintenance, but not no-maintenance. That stupid smirk lit up his face again. So, naturally, I had to make things worse.

Dragging the band out of my hair, I shook my

head and loosened the full effect of my blonde mane on him. I crossed my legs and leaned back coyly. "Is that better?" Then I gave him a little wink and a pout.

I waited for the witty comeback. Or even a witless one. But he just looked at me for the longest time. It got to be too much. "I have to go to class," I said

"Yeah, me too."

Again I waited. Because he was still standing in front of me. I sat up, shifting my weight to make it obvious he was in the way.

And still nothing.

I picked up his pen and tossed it to the other side of the room. "You dropped your pen."

Finally spurred to action, he retrieved his ballpoint, and I took the opportunity to slink off the table and to the door. Whatever game he was playing, I needed to...well, insert some appropriate sports metaphor here because I don't know any.

Wednesday afternoon, I opened my heart.

Please, you can't seriously think I'm getting all mushy on you.

I opened my interview assignment, written in calligraphy on a big pink heart. Somebody on my staff had way too much time on their hands.

The Salad Bowl.
Lane four. 6:30

The Salad Bowl was the only bowling alley in town. The newest owners were Mormon and took out the liquor bar and turned it into a salad bar. It's a good looking spread, but the smell of feet and rented shoes was still too overpowering for me to want to eat salad in there. Anyway, it looked like I had an hour of bowling to get through regardless of how it smelled.

That Foster must really hate me. You know it had to be his idea. All I really wanted to do was go home and curl up with an old Philip Marlowe movie and pretend I was a hard-boiled private detective instead of a teenage girl going on a date. Why couldn't I have been born Humphrey Bogart?

My car felt up to the drive, so I got to the Salad Bowl on my own. Which was good because I really didn't want to have Foster dropping me off on any more dates.

I mean interviews.

Wednesday nights were not a league night, so the place was pretty quiet. They had installed a new sound system, or maybe I could just hear the music better since it was dead. At any rate, catchy pop tunes poured out of the speakers and the walls were refreshed in new paint. It almost made me want to bowl. I still just didn't want to eat any salad.

One lanky boy sat in the booth on lane four, both arms stretched out to his sides, like he was making a point that he wasn't watching the door. His hair, jet black, looked a little long in the back, but not unmanageable. It was black enough that I thought maybe he dyed it. Judging from the stripes on the long-sleeve tee under his black tee, I guess him to be just this side of emo.

He stood as I approached the lane, turning slowly, and whoa…hello…Abercrombie & Fitch Boy. His blue eyes pierced the all the parts of my brain that controlled my girly hormones.

Smitten, meet the girl formerly known as Layney.

"Hi, I'm Lay—"

He held my hand in both of his. "I know exactly who you are Layney Logan, which is why I agreed to this to begin with. I'm Micah."

"You know who I am?"

"I've seen you around." His coal lashes swept down and he blushed sweetly as he smiled. "I've always liked your column in the *Follower*. I'm glad you guys haven't given up on the newspaper."

Huh.

I'd never been so close to a guy who was so…beautiful…before. My endorphins were singing. Like…opera songs. It felt similar to the time that I jumped off a cliff to get the story with the Olympic diver who was an alumnus of our school. I even liked Micah's eyebrow piercing, and I'm not usually into body jewelry.

I declined his offer to get us drinks or snacks, so we sat on the hard plastic bench and didn't even pretend to be interested in bowling.

"Why haven't I seen you at school?" I asked. Because I would have remembered. Trust me. I'm not sure teeth are supposed to be that white, but it worked for him.

"I'm probably not there as much as I should be." He smiled, wickedly even.

"So what do you do that's so important you have to cut class?"

"I skate."

Sk8er boy? Seriously? "Oh."

He rolled his eyes. "You're one of *those* people. Skateboarding isn't a crime."

I pursed my lips and gave him what I like to call

my "mom" look while I waggled my finger in front of him. "Maybe not, but I believe cutting class is."

He laughed, picking up my hand like he had every right to it. Of course, I didn't stop him. "My absences are excused. I skate competitively. I travel a lot."

"Oh." Jeez Layney. Stick your foot in it, why dontcha? "Sorry about the whole judgmental thing. Not one of my best character traits." And coupled with my lack of patience, probably why I don't have many friends outside of the paper.

Micah, still playing my fingers despite the signed contract, waited for me to make eye contact before he said, "I hope you remember that when I tell you the next thing."

Please don't let it be drugs. Please?

"I'm a sophomore."

My face fell.

I might have preferred drugs.

A sophomore?

"I was afraid of that. You don't like younger guys, do you?" He continued playing with my fingers.

"To be honest, I don't care for high school guys in general, not just the younger ones. I don't date."

"At all?"

"I've dated a few college guys, but for the most part I'm sort of married to the paper. It feels like cheating if I think about boys when I should be investigating something."

"Sounds a little lonely." He rubbed his knuckles gently up and down my arm.

"I find journalism fulfilling."

"Layney, I love skating. It's a passion—I get that. But it doesn't replace other passions. You should make room for human beings too."

I pulled my arm away from him. He didn't even know me. "Now who's being judgmental?"

"Sorry." Slumping into his seat, he blew his bangs out of his eyes. "Did I screw it up already?"

I mimicked his posture and stared at the lane in front of us, all the pins at one end, set up in perfect alignment just waiting for someone to come along and knock them all down.

And I thought I didn't know any sports metaphors.

I flipped my wrist. "According to my calculations, I have to suffer through forty-eight more minutes of your attention anyway." I shrugged. "That's probably plenty of time to change your luck, right?"

Micah dazzled me with his smile. God, why did he have to be a sophomore? I wanted to reach over and push his hair out of his eyes, but that would be wrong, right?

Right?

"I don't know if forty-eight minutes is long enough. I might have to plead special circumstances and get another date."

"Sorry, buddy. Rules are rules. You get sixty minutes and a no-contact order until after the story and calendar are published."

"I'm pretty good at rule bending."

I made a promise to myself to watch that boy skate sometime. I bet he was fabulous. "I get that impression about you."

"It's pretty big of you to sacrifice yourself like this for the paper. Having to date twelve guys. I bet no girls in school want to trade places with you or anything."

I detected a note of sarcasm. "You have no idea. I

think it just shows my commitment to the paper."

He leaned in so close that I could see the specks of navy in his blue, blue eyes. "I've got something that your newspaper doesn't have."

"Yeah, what's that?"

He leaned back into the same position I found him in. "A pierced tongue."

4 CHAPTER FOUR

Mr. March

MY staff, minus the two we'd just lost due to their lack of faith in producing a newspaper from thin air (or more likely their realization that Foster wasn't interested in hooking up), assembled around the table, once again in an argument. Foster wasn't grinning for once. In fact, he'd been pretty quiet the last two days. You'd think I'd be thrilled, but it made me nervous.

And just a hint concerned. I'm human, all right? Just because I hated him didn't mean I wanted bad things to happen to him. Or at least not heinously bad things.

I stood up and brought my fingers up like I was going to whistle. Okay, so I didn't really know how to do that, but nobody else knew that. And it worked; they shut up and let me speak. "How about we try this one at a time? Elden, what happened at the student council meeting?"

"Mr. Haney told us that that effective November 1st, any cell phone seen in students' hands during school hours would be confiscated. The device could then be picked up only by a parent and after a fifteen dollar fine was paid." Then he added, "It isn't fair."

"Fair?" I asked.

"It seems unconstitutional to me," a girl named Evie added.

My eyes wanted to roll so badly—but I simply closed them until the feeling passed. "It's been two years since I've had U.S. history, but I'm pretty sure the constitution didn't promise the right to bear cell phones." I blew my bangs out of my eyes. "Let's try this again, only this time, let's pretend we're reporters. Elden?"

"It isn't fair!" Elden chimed in. Again. "And my name is Alden. Still."

Whoops.

"Fair means nothing," I said. "Lots of things aren't fair. Try again. Where's the story?"

Blank faces. And a very bored co-chief at the other end of the table, spinning his pen through his fingers and staring out the window.

Fine. I stood. "Is the seizure legal?"

"How would we know?" asked Elden, or Alden, whatever.

"We find out. That's what we do. That whole reporting thing and all." Energized, I continued. "Eld—Alden, interview Haney. And I'm changing your name to Frank. Find out where the mandate came from. School board? Teachers' lounge? Then research city and state statutes for limits of power. Do they have the jurisdiction to impose fines? Is it lawful to confiscate student property if it isn't illegal or dangerous? What recourse do parents and students have?"

Frank scribbled furiously, and I began pacing. "Evie, interview a few teachers. Get some opinions from their trenches, but try to find a sampling of for and against. It's important that we show both sides, or the story becomes opinion not reporting." I stopped at Foster's seat and kicked his chair.

He sighed but relented. "Chelsea, get student reactions. Look especially for alternative ideas from the study body that might satisfy the issues that led to the ruling. Is there a compromise?"

While he was speaking, he held up his right hand holding a pink slip of paper. I snatched it from his fingers and strode to the other side of the room to open it in peace.

The Paint Pot.
Table three. 7:00.

Seriously? Foster didn't look at me, but he must have felt my glare, because the grin that crossed his face was the one he reserved for tormenting me.

The Paint Pot was one of those places where you paint your own...well, pot or mug or plate or whatever. They bake it for you in their kiln and then you have an immortalized piece of pottery to commemorate...your blind date with Mr. March.

I'm not one of those people who saves little pieces of memorabilia. The past belongs right where it is as far as I'm concerned. My favorite holiday is New Year's Day—I never have a problem saying goodbye to the old year and hello to the new.

The crew filed out, leaving Foster and me alone. Again. I didn't understand why that made me feel so weird lately. I mean, the only feelings I harbored for my lost relationship with Foster were not the kind that make your stomach feel full of butterflies. Maybe a rock tumbler full of stones…but not butterflies.

"Was the Paint Pot your idea?" I asked.

"Actually, no. The girls are being surprisingly independent on this venture. And they are taking it very seriously."

I checked out his grandpa shirt. "But the Salad Bowl—that was all you, wasn't it?"

He gifted me with the smile signifying another point for Team Hell. "Yeah. I remembered how much you used to love bowling."

"I hate bowling."

"I know. I just told you I remembered."

I sucked in a deep breath and tried to think of my happy place. Unfortunately, we were already standing in my happy place and it was less than joyful.

"How are the photo shoots going? Any proofs?"

Mr. Self-Satisfied snickered. "Don't you worry about the photo shoots. Your job is clear—we just need you to stand around and look pretty for a while."

I was about to berate him when he stopped me.

"Or at least fair-looking, if you think you can manage it."

It hurt. I knew he was only being mean because I was poking him about having to take beefcake photos—well, that and the fact that he was evil. But it still hurt.

I stormed out, riding the waves of my righteous anger for the rest of the day.

Arriving at the Paint Pot ten minutes early still didn't get me there before my date. I peered in the window and saw a very big linebacker sitting at a table already. I wonder if Foster didn't tell the guys to be there at a different time than me just so I wouldn't have a chance to get comfortable with my surroundings first.

My pocket buzzed. I pulled out my phone but didn't recognize the number.

"Hello?"

"Hey. It's Micah."

My heart skipped a beat. "How did you get my number?"

"I can't give you my sources, Ms. Reporter. I heard you had another date tonight and just didn't want you to forget about me."

Like that was going to happen. "You are breaking the rules," I said sternly through a smile.

"Maybe we should meet in person so you can chastise me properly."

"I'm on a date with another boy. That would be the ultimate etiquette breach."

Micah sighed. "I'm in Toronto anyway. Wish me luck?"

"Oh." Heart, meet pit of stomach. So far away? "Yeah, of course. Good luck shredding the pipe or whatever I'm supposed to say."

Somehow, I felt his smile through the phone. "Have a nice date, Layney."

Huh. Boys were more complicated than I thought.

I turned my phone off, just in case, and pulled open the door to meet bachelor number three.

BN3 actually stood up when I got to his table. All three hundred pounds of him. He was close to a foot taller and had about two hundred pounds on me—but he was the opposite of scary. Don't laugh, but he had Santa Claus eyes. They twinkled.

"Hi Layney. I'm Tyler."

I couldn't stop smiling, and I had no idea why. Tyler put me at ease immediately. He was like…a cup of cocoa and a book on a snowy day.

"Thanks for agreeing to the interview—I mean date." We sat down and I inspected the plain mug in front of me. "Head's up. I'm not going to impress you with my artistic ability tonight. I'm better with written words than pictures."

He laughed. From his belly—again, like Santa, if Santa were a Polynesian high school student. "It'll be fun."

An employee came to our table and explained the process to us, and then left us to our own devices. While she talked, I took the room in, trying to come up with the words that could describe it. Kitschy? Perky? There was an abundance of blue and yellow gingham, and the employee sported some serious apron flair.

"Do you play football, Tyler?" Because, duh.

"I play church league, but they chose me for the calendar because I'm in the high school choir."

"The choir?"

He nodded. "I know most people think I'd be better at football or sumo wrestling—but I really enjoy singing and playing the piano."

"I don't sing."

"Ever?"

"Not in front of anyone." I shivered, pretending I was cold—but really, that was how much I hated singing in front of people. "What do you like to sing?"

"I like the old stuff—Sinatra, Sammy Davis Jr., Dean Martin..."

The image of Tyler singing songs my great-grandmother listened too struck me as odd, yet in a really refreshing way. And I doubt he had to put up with too much teasing. He may have a smooth voice, but he was still built for damage.

The clean paintbrushes on the table mocked me with their unsullied bristles. "I have no idea how to start this."

"You're a lot more uptight than I thought you were."

That surprised me until I realized he was right. Everything about me was rigid—my stiff arms, my severe posture. I exhaled and shook out my limbs. "Sorry. I don't know why I'm so tense."

"It's just a mug. If you want, you can put a dot on it and call it done. No pressure."

Tyler, on the other hand, busily ran his brush over the mug in front of him. No pressure. Hah. My plain white cup blinked at me like a fully lit neon sign that flashed *Failure! Failure!* "What are you putting on yours?"

"I can't tell you. You'll have to wait until it's done."

I must have picked up and set down everything in front of me at least twice. When I drummed my fingers on the edge, he set down his own brush and leaned back into his chair.

I expected some sort of reprimand for my nervous energy or lack of participation in the artistic portion of the evening's program. Instead, Tyler asked me, "What actress would you pick to play you in the movie version of your life?"

"I can honestly say that I've never thought of that. Can I be Humphrey Bogart?"

"No."

"Does she have to be living?"

"It would make it easier to cast her in the role, but I suppose for you we can make an exception."

"Fine. I'll play it your way. That girl who plays Veronica Mars."

"You kind of look like her."

"What about you? Who plays Tyler in the movie of your life?"

"Elvis Presley."

"Nice. I think people would spend the $12.50 to see Elvis and Veronica Mars on a date in a pottery-painting store, don't you?"

"Box-office hit written all over it."

We chatted some more and he told me lovely stories about growing up in Hawaii, where his grandparents still lived. The way he described the fresh pineapple made my mouth water, and I could almost smell coconuts. Tyler came from a long line of storytellers, and I really believe he could carry on the tradition.

He still wouldn't let me see the mug, though, even going so far as to sneak it up the store employee. I assumed that meant that I would end up keeping the one he made for me, which meant the one I had in front of me was going to have to be for him.

I picked up the brush again when he went to restroom and painted the words:

I went on a date with Veronica Mars, and all I got was this lousy coffee mug.

The nice lady came and got it from me, explaining

that the King of Rock and Roll already made arrangements to pick them up next week and deliver mine to me.

When Tyler sat down, I smiled.

"Why are you smiling?" he asked. "Not that I'm complaining. You don't look constipated anymore at least."

"I don't know," I answered. "I think I just like you. Is that weird?"

"Yeah."

I didn't have a lot of friends. Okay, I didn't have any friends. I mean, I wasn't like scary loner in a black trench coat; I did function and interact with people. And people interested me—as a writer, how could they not? But I didn't have anyone my own age to share confidences with. I talked to Mr. Blake about career planning and stuff like that. My mom consoled me when I needed to vent about school. Through the years, I would hang out with the upperclassmen on the paper staff on the weekends—but now that I was the upperclassmen, I was sort of alone.

Which normally didn't bother me so much. But just hanging out with Tyler made me feel—normal, I guess. His easygoing manner suited me. That he would never make me hold his hair while throwing up or borrow my favorite shirt and never return it made him even more appealing.

"I'll tell you why I'm smiling if you tell me what you put on that mug."

Santa Elvis just smiled.

"Fine. I guess we both have our secrets. Do you want to come over on Sunday and watch football with me after you get home from church?"

"You like football?"

"I love football. Well, not really, but I'll watch it with you anyway."

"I thought there was some kind of rule…"

"I'm good at bending rules. Here's the thing—I've decided that you are going to be the closest thing to a BFF I'll allow myself to have. Whether you like it or not, we're buddies now."

"Okay, psycho girl. But if you start wearing your hair like mine and pilfering my clothes like that *Single White Female* movie, we're breaking up."

5 CHAPTER FIVE

Mr. April

WAVES of nostalgia crested over me as I opened the heavy door and stepped into the darkened space. This corner was always best rushed through. At least it used to be. Once you ran through it, down the slightly creepy corridor, a magical kingdom awaited.

In four years, little had changed. Lights bounced off the walls in green, red, blue, and white. A disconcerting mesh of fragrance permeated the air consisting of nacho cheese, watermelon bubble gum, and feet. Music pumped through an ancient sound system while giggles and screams bounced off the walls, and a disco ball oversaw the mayhem from its perch in the middle of it all.

I hadn't been roller-skating in four years.

I showed up half an hour early hoping to get my bearings on the wheels before I embarrassed myself in front of Mr. April. Standing in line to trade my shoes in for skates, a smile stretched across my face listening to the girls around me.

"Jake told Lissa that Connor wants to ask me out, but every time I try to talk to Connor, he just says he has to go now."

"My mom said I can't wear eye shadow until next year. That is so lame."

"Did you see who Parker was talking to after school yesterday? Ohmigawd, I totally thought they broke up already."

The conversations, cute at first because they reminded me of my own misspent middle school days, quickly became tiresome by the time I reached the counter. Makeup, boys, and gossip. Unfortunately, I'm not convinced that the chat would be so different if it were seventeen-year-olds in line instead of thirteen-year-olds.

Lacing up my boots filled me with apprehension but also a strange warmth—a glow even. Some of my best memories took place inside these walls. The rink used to be my favorite haunt.

Jimmy Foster's too.

An ache quickly replaced the glow. The pang of regret, the sorrow of loss. Those days were a lot simpler. We spent seventh and most of eighth grade here. Together. In fact, we spent every possible minute of every day together, as well as a few illicit nights (not that illicit) in which we had to sneak out of our houses and meet in the dead of night just because we couldn't stand to be apart for very long.

I used to really love Jimmy Foster.

My heart crinkled at the memories, and I tried to brush them off. Remembering the way we were wasn't going to help me deal with the way we are.

Someday, when I didn't have to manage—daily—the satanic version of the boy he'd become, I'd let my heart have its way. Until then, a fondness for my first crush—no, it was more than that—my first love, would have to wait.

A boy plopped down on the bench beside me, so I straightened automatically. I wasn't supposed to meet my date for fifteen more minutes, but since he was the only guy in the room over the age of fourteen and smiling at me, I realized that once again, I'd underestimated Foster's desire to keep me on edge by having my escorts be early.

I recognized this date. Dean Darnell was the campus celeb in the way that only the most annoying popular kids get to be. Nobody challenged his run at Homecoming King, though who else would want it? Dean was the kind of guy who blow-dried his blond shaggy Efron hair every morning, and I'd bet money that he had a skin-care regimen. He wore his two-hundred-dollar jeans with the same ease that he climbed into his shiny black Hummer. Those kinds of boys practice being effortless.

As only the very entitled would dare, he snaked his arm behind me and lounged in his seat, probably waiting for me to gush about the privilege of his company.

"Hey, Dean."

"Hey, Laynster."

"How are you?" I asked, pretending to care. We weren't exactly friends, but we had friends in common. Well, as close to friends as I had. I didn't hate Dean; I just really didn't care how he was one way or the other.

"I'll be better when we get out of here." He didn't

have skates on, and he hadn't rented any either.

"Sorry, you'll have to suffer for one hour. Where are your skates?"

Dean leaned in close, way too close. Like get-out-of-my-bubble-bad-man too close. "You don't seriously want to stay here, do you? We could go for a drive."

The scent of alcohol on his breath drifted my way, and with it a deluge of unwanted memories landslided their way through my head. Random blips of ugly things I wanted to forget threw themselves into my path, throwing me off-kilter. The smell of whiskey...the heaviness of a hand...the spinning of the room. Things I hadn't thought about in a long time.

I stood up quickly, forgetting I was on skates. Dean rose also, righting me as I slipped. "Thanks. Um, you better go get your skates. I think there's a rule..."

"Everyone has to pay for skate rental. There's no rule that you have to put them on your feet. Besides, we can't really get to know each other here. Let's go for a drive. C'mon."

My gut twisted and I grew light-headed. I'd never had a panic attack before, and I sure didn't want to start in a skating rink. My world spiraled to a pinpoint of light and my hands grew clammy.

"Are you okay? Do you need some air?" He reached for my hand, but I shook him off. "Okay, okay." He held his hands in mock surrender. "We'll stay here." Reaching into his jacket, he pulled out a flask. "Besides, I brought the party to us."

We can have a party right here. Just you and me.

The rink pitched sideways as that voice from my

past rang out in my mind as clear as the day he said it.

No, clearer. Clarity was one thing I had lacked that night.

My face flushed hot and cold and I fought the urge to throw up or run away. I couldn't be scared. I don't do scared. I stared at a candy wrapper on the floor until the world leveled again.

"Put the booze away, Dean." Hugging my arms to my chest, irrational fear and anger coursed through me. Pride, perhaps my biggest flaw, was also the only one that kept me from falling part all these years, and I'd be damned if I lost my sense of self now, after all this time.

He pocketed the flask and his face pinched into a worried look. "Are you sure you're okay? You look kinda pale."

He grabbed my elbow, but this time he held on when I tried to shrug out of his grasp. Having all these feelings was sort of foreign to me, and having him clutch at me sort of popped my cork. I yanked my arm wildly, and when he saw the look in my eyes, he released me immediately, causing me to reel backward on the stupid wheels on my feet. Dean reached for me again to stop my fall, only he got slammed from behind by another skater who came out of nowhere.

The skater pushed Dean into the wall, pinning him in place. "Sorry, man," he said but didn't back off. "I lost my balance."

I grabbed the bench and steadied myself again but recognized the voice. "Foster?" What was he doing here? "What are you doing here?"

Dean growled at him. "Get off me, dude."

Foster had braced his arm across Dean's chest just

below his neck. "Sorry, my bad. Haven't been skating in a few years. Are you both okay?" He spoke to me over his shoulder. "Are you all right, Logan?"

"I'm fine." Oh my God. Was he pinning Dean to the wall for me? "Foster, let him go."

"So your date is over, then, Dean." It wasn't a question; it was a statement. Things were definitely veering toward Testosteronelandia between the two boys. I'd never seen Foster like this.

Dean pushed back and Foster let go. As Dean brushed off his clothes, he answered, "The date just started. We've got an hour."

"I don't think you do." Foster planted his feet so that he was between Dean and me. "I think the date is over now."

This new Foster surprised me. I suppose he looked taller because of the skates, but he also looked more menacing than I remembered. And trust me—roller skates don't usually up the intimidating quota for guys.

Which of course meant that Dean had to ante in his most threatening pose. "I'm not on a date with you, Foster. So back off."

The boys took a step (*roll?*) closer to each other and turned all kinds of primal-looking. The shock of it snapped me out of my earlier meltdown and into fix-it mode because if I didn't do something fast, there was going to be a fight.

"Foster." I reached for his sleeve.

With his other hand, he pointed to Dean. "What part of not touching her was unclear in the contract?"

"Relax. I wasn't groping her. I was keeping her from falling on her ass."

"Hey!" I blurted. Well, he had a point. Still, I

needed to call a halt to the fight about to happen.

Despite not recognizing the song that was playing, I clutched Foster's arm. "Oh my God! I love this song. Let's skate."

He didn't come willingly at first, but I tugged hard enough that he got the point. We stumbled toward the opening in the rink wall, mostly because he refused to lose eye contact with Dean and half walked, half rolled backward as Dean strolled backward out the door.

I'd never pretended to understand testosterone.

As soon as my wheels touched the smooth floor, I worried that I'd made a huge mistake. I should have let them fight it out while I put my shoes back on instead. Foster held me up for a few seconds until I found my center. We started rolling without speaking until I felt myself falling back into place, piece by piece. Like riding a bike, to overuse a cliché, something a good reporter is never supposed to do.

"Why are you here tonight?" I asked. The roller rink wasn't really high on places Foster would like to spend time now that he wasn't thirteen.

"You're welcome, of course," he answered.

"No, really. Why?"

"I've gone on all your dates."

My lovely rhythm suddenly faltered. "What? Why?"

"For times like tonight." Foster put his hand out to catch my fall, just in case. "Look, I know you get off casting me as the bad guy in your little dramas, and most of the time I'm happy play the part. That doesn't mean I'd let you go out with twelve strangers without backup."

As my mind whirled into action, my motor skills

kicked in and I was able to fall into the easy gliding of my youth. Because I couldn't concentrate on my feet and my mortification at the same time. He'd been on every date? "Where? How?"

"Usually in the manager's office. I stay out of the way. Before you ask, I didn't tell you because I was hoping it wouldn't be necessary. I figured you might be self-conscious if you knew someone was watching—"

"Spying."

"Watching."

We cruised another loop with no words. I was just fresh out of them.

I don't think I'd been at the roller rink for more than half an hour, but I felt like I'd been put through one of those old-fashioned wringers they used to use to wash clothes. At some point, I was going to have to apologize to Dean for turning all wacky on him and letting my partner cause a fight, but I didn't want to think of that at the moment. Nor did I want to dwell on my little episode brought on by the smell of the whiskey on Dean's breath.

That left either how I felt about Foster going caveman when I felt threatened or the bittersweet nostalgia I was feeling for days of yore.

Neither were safe zones.

"This place hasn't changed much." Foster's gaze swept over my face briefly, and in it I remembered a very different boy and a very different girl. The young boy with less cynical eyes and a quicker smile.

What would I tell them now if I could go back and give little Layney and little Jimmy advice about treading the treacherous waters of the eighth grade? Not that they would listen. Why would they? Layney

Logan and Jimmy Foster would have LOL'd their way across the rink. Everybody knew they were rock solid. The L word had been passed between them. Two bases had been stolen. He'd given her a heart necklace for Valentine's Day. She promised third base when they got to high school.

They were in love.

"No, it's still the same here," I answered. The memories tasted like an unripe berry dipped in sugar—sweet with a bitter ever after. Still, I smiled. The music pumped out Beyoncé, my body remembered the groove, and the movement felt good—like a stretch after a nap.

He smiled too, loosening up. "I'd forgotten how fun skating is."

"You going to start coming back every weekend?"

"Maybe."

"Careful. You'll be eighteen soon. They'll label you a pedophile."

"Seriously. It's fun, right? You're having a good time?"

I cast him a sidelong glance and decided to dam my first instinct to resort to sarcasm. "I'm not…wishing I was someplace else right now."

Foster clutched his chest. "Don't phunk with my heart, Logan."

I answered with a playful punch. "You'll need to get one first. I hear they sell them at Evil 'R Us. You have an account there, don't you? Maybe you can pick one up on the 'still beating/just pulled from a sacrifice' aisle."

"Do you have any idea how expensive those are? Even with my discount—"

The song ended, but instead of immediately sliding

into the next one, the lights dimmed, and the announcement proclaimed "couples-only skate."

We hit an awkward patch that was hard to navigate, and clearly neither of us knew what to do. Our past collided with our present and the two of us were trapped in the wreckage. Leaving the rink would mean giving too much importance to a should-be-forgotten childhood pastime. Staying meant...well, the same thing probably.

Foster kept his eyes forward but silently reached for my hand.

Children all around us paired off. At first, holding hands with Foster was like driving someone else's car—everything seems weird and wrong, but you still know how to drive it, and and after a minute or two, you don't have to think about it. You just are.

Transported to another time, another lifetime, we eased into our old selves. Never more aware of his body, I allowed myself to sync to his movements and found that we still made a pretty good team.

"Do you remember how to skate backward?" he asked me.

"Huh?" Then as he tugged, I answered, "No Foster, don't."

Too late, he swept me into our old waltz-pose and I didn't lose a beat as I began skating backward while he held me. Exhilarated, I felt that zing racing through me, just like when we argue, only we weren't at cross-purposes for once.

Back in the years of our roller-skating glory, Foster and I spent so much time on wheels that we had our own routines, especially for couples' skate. Minus lifts, jumps, and bedazzled matching costumes, of course. More or less, they were just patterns we'd developed over time. Except that when we were kids, the weight of his hand on my hip didn't reboot my nervous system in quite the same way.

After a few minutes, he spun me around until we faced the same direction again with his right arm behind me, holding my right hand and resting on my hip, and my arm extended in front of him, holding his left hand. That we didn't trip over each other's feet amazed me. When he moved so that he was behind me, I instinctively tilted my head because he used to rest his chin on my shoulder. We let go of our hands, and his arms crossed in front of me, pulling me in tightly. We were one person, if only for a few seconds.

And all it took was one kid tripping to undo the moment.

The fall happened in super slow-mo. Not the kid's fall. My fall.

The kid tripped. I saw it happen and instantly knew he would be my own downfall. Literally. Foster tried to spin around, so he made first contact, tripping on the boy's skate and landing hard on his butt with me following right after. I thunked my knee hard, but Foster broke my fall. Unfortunately, he couldn't also shield me from the couple right behind us, who both toppled and landed mostly on me.

Disengaging and getting upright proved to be a lot more awkward than even the falling. Being manhandled by Jimmy Foster at the skating rink used to happen two or three times a week. The difference was he used to do it on purpose so he didn't apologize when he brushed against my breasts. This time, he blushed and stammered.

By the time we made it to the benches, we were

both war weary and said very little while we unlaced the boots. We limped our way to the counter and then finally to the parking lot.

"Well, there's my car," I stated, even though it was obvious. "Where is yours?"

"I parked a block away so you wouldn't spot me."

It figures. "That's right. I almost forgot to be upset about the spying part. Thanks for reminding me. Expect that I'll be angry with you on Monday morning."

Foster shrugged. "I always expect you'll be angry at me on Monday mornings."

He declined the offer of a ride to his car but offered to stay long enough to make sure mine started. As I limped away, I could tell he was staring at my ass by the burn.

Funny that rather than making me angry, it made me smile. Insert chapter five text here.

6 CHAPTER SIX

Mr. May

"I JUST GOT A BLUE slip to see Maple," I told Tyler, who was on the other end of my cell phone call.

"What did you do?" he asked.

"I have no idea. So we can talk more about my near panic attack later, I guess."

"You just don't want to talk about it all."

"It was no big deal. I have to go."

And it wasn't a big deal. I just had a moment of panic that sorted itself out. Talking about it wasn't going to change how I felt last night or how I felt in eighth grade. Stuff happens; move on.

The secretary was on the phone and waved me into the office. Ms. Maple, our vice-principal, rose from her seat when I entered her office. She'd stuffed herself into a lime green suit today. It went really well with her brassy red bun. I'd watched *Facts of Life* on Nick at Nite before. She was Mrs. Garrett's evil twin.

"Miss Logan."

"Ms. Maple."

She indicated to a chair. "Please have a seat." Which meant sit whether you want to or not. She didn't waste time and started speaking as we both sat down. "I'll get right to the point, Layney. The district is not happy with your little newspaper club causing so much trouble about the cell phone issue. The topic is already heated enough."

My little newspaper club? I leaned toward her over the desk. "Are you referring to the journalists of a highly regarded periodical asking questions? I don't see how that is causing trouble, Miss Maple. I see that as students thinking critically, something your staff attempts to teach us every day."

"I'll remind you that there is no longer a 'highly regarded periodical' as you say. You are now participating in a campus club and will adhere to the directives of ..." She paused briefly as she noticed a memo pad on her desk. Her eyes darted back to me quickly. "The directives of the administration, or we'll shut you down."

Nonchalantly—which, by the way, is very telling to bloodhounds like me—she palmed her memo pad and slid it closer to her side of the desk.

What was she going to do with it, and why didn't she want me to see it? "Ms. Maple, my staff is not out to cause trouble. There is a legitimate story here. Not only do students deserve to know if their rights are being violated, but they also need to know if they are not. We are conducting interviews with key members of your staff as well as..." This time I paused. She ripped the top page of her memo pad off and folded it in her hand several times before pocketing it.

Interesting. "As well as members of the governing body of the school. Your bosses, I guess you could say."

She arched an eyebrow. I'm not afraid to give credit—she does it better than I do. "You are not conducting interviews. You're conducting witch hunts." She tucked the pad between a couple of folders and then folded her hands in front of her again. "Do you think we came about this decision lightly?"

No, but I did think she was hiding something from me. "Of course not. The paper will lay out the story in an unbiased way, I assure you."

"There is no paper, Layney."

"The *Follower* is not dead." I stood. "We are coming back and we'll be even better than before."

"You have no print press. And don't think you can use school materials to Xerox your little newsletter, either."

Getting angry would not help. In fact, that is probably what she wanted me to do. Then she could punish me and maybe even bury the *Follower* forever. The question remained—why? "There is such a thing as free speech still, isn't there?"

Ms. Maple stood. "This isn't a democracy. This is a high school. You'd best remember that if you want to keep your club on school grounds."

I fished out my recorder. Luckily, I had one that didn't double as my cell phone. "I'd like to make sure I understood you correctly, Ms. Maple. Is it okay if I record the rest of our conversation so that I can relay accurate information back to the other members of my little club?"

She glared at me. You'll have to take my word for

it because it won't show up on the audio. I sat back down and turned my weapon on. If she wasn't going to say no, I was going to assume she meant yes.

"Ms. Maple, is it true that you do not want the newspaper to cover the story regarding the recent student cell phone mandates because you feel the issue is too heated? Therefore, in your opinion, stifling an honest exchange of information will be better for the school board than full disclosure?"

"That is not what I said."

"I see. So you *don't* intend to shut down the *Follower* if we pursue our first-amendment right to free speech?"

She pursed her lips like a constipated fish. "If the newspaper club follows all the school rules regarding campus groups, then of course it is free to remain a school activity."

I sent her my perky smile. The one that gives Foster hives. "Perhaps you'd like to give me an exclusive. Tell me—"

I was interrupted by her cell phone ringing. People would pay good money for this kind of irony.

"Do you need to get that?" I asked. "It's okay if you do. We still have six weeks until November first." She knit her brow in confusion. "I'm assuming that since the regulations came down because cellular devices were detracting from children's education, that means all teachers and staff members will also have to abide by the rule, right?"

"I think you better get back to class, Ms. Logan."

"Okey dokey." I bounced off my seat and to the door. "Thanks for all your help with the story."

For the rest of the day, I was distracted by the secret memo incident. She really didn't want me to see that note, so of course I had to find a way get the goods.

After school, I skipped out of our newspaper meeting a little early. As I used my "cartoon classic-sneaky-walk"—you know, the one Shaggy and Scooby use when they are trying to hide from a ghost—I got almost all the way to Ms. Maple's desk when I felt the hand on my shoulder.

"What the hell are you doing?"

I'll admit, I also performed the "cartoon I-am-a-statue" move for a second. Then I realized it was Foster.

I pivoted toward him and shushed him. "I'm investigating if you must know," I whispered.

"Investigating what? How did you get in here? Bobby pin or credit card?"

I held up a key. "I have friends in very low places." He rolled his eyes, but I know he had to be impressed. I'd bet another date at the rink he only wished he had keys to the administrators' offices.

The undeniable clip-clop of heels sounded in the hall, and my whole high school career flashed before my eyes. I'd gotten into a few scrapes over the years, but getting caught breaking and entering into the vice-principal's office was going to be a little deeper of a cut. My panicked brain started me toward her desk, but Foster grabbed me and hauled me into her closet with him. The closet was good. Better than the behind-the-desk I was shooting for. Unless, of course, Ms. Maple had come back for her coat.

The pitch black of the closet didn't exactly make me happy. I'm not claustrophobic or afraid of the dark, but I was actually glad I wasn't alone, even if it was Foster with me.

We'd pointedly ignored each other most of the day, not wanting rehash the whole couples'-skate fiasco. We shared one brief moment during lunch when we caught each other wincing as we sat down in the newsroom, reminding us of our mutual roller-skating injuries. I offered to track down a doughnut pillow for him to sit on, and he offered me a box of tissue to stuff my bra with.

So things were pretty much back to normal.

Except for the fact that we were hiding in a dark closet. There were boxes or something on the floor to our right, so we had to mush together with me in front and both of us facing the same direction. We could hear Ms. Maple ratting around in her desk drawer for something while she talked on her cell.

"Oh there it is!" she exclaimed. She jabbered on, her voice getting closer and closer to our hiding spot. Foster and I both pushed back farther. We heard her hand on the door handle, so I squinted my eyes closed and turned my face into his chest.

We were so busted. And what the hell was that pushing into my backside?

My eyes popped open and I gasped. Foster covered my mouth with his hand. Just then, Ms. Maple said to her phone, "If my head weren't attached I'd have left it here too. You are not going to believe what I just did. I almost looked in my closet for the coat I'm already wearing." She laughed, and then her voice got quieter and the office door closed behind her.

The lock clicked and we both let out our breath. We spilled out of the closet and I swung around to confront him.

He flashed me the universal don't-say-it hand sign.

"Not a word."

"I can't believe you. You had a...a...a stiffy!"

He blushed furiously, reminding me he really was redheaded. "Look, I'm a guy. Your ass was touching my groin. Of course I'm going to pop a boner. It's a natural reaction."

"Yeah, but..." But what? He was right. I just assumed he'd be immune to that sort of reaction when it came to me.

"Can we just finish this secret mission now?" he asked. "Why are we here?"

"*We* are here because you were spying on me again. *I* am here because Ms. Maple was acting very suspicious during our meeting today. She is hiding something." Striding to her desk, I plucked her memo pad from its hiding spot, vindicated that it was still there. "She didn't want me to see whatever she had written on this pad."

Foster joined me at the desk with a keychain flashlight, and I pulled a pencil from my pocket. Just like Nancy Drew, I rubbed the lead over the paper to reveal traces of the note left behind.

"B-i-k," Foster read aloud. "I can't make it out. What does that say?"

As the words revealed themselves, I dropped the pencil like it was hot. Ms. Maple wasn't being blackmailed into enforcing the stupid phone rule. She wasn't hiding the location of a secret treasure or dead body either. She was getting a bikini wax on Wednesday at four.

Personally, I could have gone my whole life without knowing Mrs. Garrett's evil twin waxes.

"My stiffy is gone."

I snorted when I laughed. "Do you suppose she

65

gets a landing strip or the Elmer Fudd?"

"Could you never ask me that again?" He rubbed his face. "Are we done now?"

"Yeah. I think I have all the information I need."

Since I knew Foster was coming anyway, I accepted his offer of a ride to my date. We did not speak of bikini lines or woodies on the way to Abby's Diner. Though we did have an interesting conversation about fonts and typefaces. Well, it was interesting to us anyway.

Mr. May revealed himself to be Steven J. Morten—at least that was how he introduced himself to me as we met across the diner table. His handshake was firm, but his skin felt on the clammy side to me.

Other than that, his appearance was unremarkable. Not quite matured yet, he carried himself like a freshman maybe. His face still had that baby-soft look to it, and behind his glasses, his eyes seemed boyish. A nice change from the last date, who thought he was more man than he really was.

Abby's Diner was a retro 50's joint and famous for their pies. Steven and I both ordered peach ala mode which gave us a great conversation starter.

I offered, "Peach is my favorite."

He replied, "I just got it because you did."

Cue uncomfortable silence.

"Do you have a favorite pie?" I asked.

"Not really."

"Oh."

Again, this really wasn't working. I looked to the surroundings for a kick-start. Nothing about Formica and chrome screamed "good conversation." The jukebox kicked out "Teenager in Love" and the night wasn't getting any younger.

"So Steven, what school clubs do you participate in?"

"Just the Spanish Club." I thought that was all he was going to say, but then he added, "But I'm really into art."

"Oh?"

He picked up a portfolio on the bench next to him. "I brought a few of my favorites. Would you like to see them?"

I had just taken a big bite of pie, so I nodded and he pushed the portfolio across the table. Upon opening to the first page, the pie in my stomach offered a repeat performance.

"Um. Wow," I mumbled. He turned the page. "These are really…" *Disgusting.* "Intense."

He turned the page again and I tried not to wince.

"They are very…" *Vulgar. Vile.* I reached for a nonthreatening word. "Vivid?"

Because the mind of Steven J. Morten was apparently a very scary place.

Each drawing was indeed intense and vivid. And the stuff of nightmares. Naked teenage girls that I recognized as cheerleaders sprawled in painful poses while being eviscerated or beheaded by demonic, hulking beasts. Page after page of death, violence, and destruction amid burning urban landscapes. I looked at Steven again, thinking I misjudged his appearance, but no, he still had that guileless young boy vibe despite the fact that his mind vomited up such detailed ugliness.

"So your favorite medium is pencil?" I asked while texting *SOS* by Braille to a demon sometimes scarier than the ones on the paper in front of me.

He nodded. "But I did do a painted mural on my bedroom wall. Hey, do you want to come to my house and see it?"

Blinking away visions of the chains and torture devices he might have awaiting for me in his bedroom, I declined. "I'm not allowed to take this date out of the restaurant. Sorry."

Steven shrugged. "Maybe some other time." His gaze shifted to something behind me. "Hey, what is Jimmy Foster doing here?"

Oh, thank God. Lucifer was going to save me. I was afraid he wasn't going to take my text seriously.

Foster stopped at our table. "Hey, guys, sorry to interrupt."

"Oh hi, Foster. What a surprise seeing you here." I smiled brightly at him even though he obviously questioned the distress call. I'm sure that by all appearances, my date with Mr. May seemed pretty tame. "Steven was just showing me his drawings. Can I show them to Foster, Steven?"

Steven pushed his glasses up further on the bridge of his nose. "Sure, I guess."

I tilted the book so Foster could get the full effect of the carnage. "Whoa." I seldom got the chance to see Foster discombobulated. If I weren't ready to retch, it would have been more enjoyable. "That is really...."

I offered, "Vivid?"

"Yeah, vivid. So sorry to cut your date short, guys, but we are having an emergency at the paper and I need Layney right now."

"An emergency? Oh no." I pushed myself out of the booth. "I'm so sorry, Steven, but I really have to go."

Foster patted Steven on the shoulder. "Good luck with your art, man. Stay and finish your pie." He grabbed my hand and pulled me toward the door.

I went gladly and without complaint. Sometimes, the devil you know really is safer.

7 CHAPTER SEVEN

Mr. June

A FEW days later I was dreading the newsroom because it was date night again and I wasn't sure if I was up to it anymore. The last two had taken their toll. The thought of seven more chilled my marrow.

I like people, kind of. I even like boys, mostly. But I was beginning to feel like that stewardess who smiles at you when you get off the plane. Behind the smile you know she really wishes she could trip someone.

Plus, I'd been having strange dreams. Not the kind where you remember the oddness—more like the kind that leave their dregs of uneasiness behind long after you wake up. Tyler told me to keep a journal next to my bed and write them down as soon as I woke up. Like I didn't keep a journal under my pillow already. Please, I am a writer. I could start an office supply store out of my car on any given day.

But the dreams vanished as soon as I opened my eyes, never staying long enough for me to catch them with my wily pen and parchment.

It was only the vague disquiet that stayed behind.

I thought about staying home sick, but Tyler was bringing my mug from our date to school. And buying me lunch. I wanted both, so I toughed it out.

As I meandered slowly across campus, I spied Micah rolling toward me. What a beautiful, beautiful boy. Rays of sun backlit him like an angel, and if I wasn't mistaken, he had two cups of coffee in a to-go tray in his hand.

He smiled and did some fancy footwork to stop rolling once he got to me. "Hey, Layney."

"Hey, Micah. Nice to see you at school for a change."

"Does that mean you miss me when I'm not here?" He passed me a coffee. "I have this extra coffee here, and it's a good thing you happened by or I would have to throw it away or something."

"This is cheating."

"No, this is coffee.

"We are supposed to be contact free."

"I had no idea I would run into you. Harmless, coincidental caffeine." Every now and then, I caught a glimpse of his tongue piercing when he spoke, and it made my tummy flutter a little. "I wasn't sure what you liked, so I got you a mocha."

I smiled graciously. I've never actually had more than a sip of a mocha, but I didn't want to hurt his feelings. "What girl doesn't like chocolate?"

I just didn't like mine with my coffee.

That must have been a good answer, because he looked pleased with himself as he smiled and puffed out his chest. "Are you going to be online after your date tonight?"

Okay. Small confession. I'd been cyberflirting with Micah since he texted me from Toronto. Nothing serious. Just a few minutes here and there and a couple winking smilies from time to time.

"I don't know. I have a calculus test tomorrow. I might have to be in full-on study mode." I checked my watch. "Speaking of my date tonight, I better go retrieve my mission from the newsroom. Thanks for the coffee."

Micah's grin turned the blood in my veins to a molten hot wax. He could melt me from the inside out, he was that hot. It's like he wafted in an air of wickedness—just a smidge, but enough to trigger all the right hormonal responses. Too bad he was only a sophomore. If I was going to break my boyfriend fast this year, he'd be my number one candidate.

But I wasn't going to, was I?

As I pondered the thought across campus and into the newsroom, it occurred to me that this dating nonsense might be poking at the soft, fleshy parts of my heart that I thought I had protected several years ago. My choice to abstain from high school relationships was deliberate and wise. It's not like my future would include anyone I dated as a teenager, so why go through the messy detour? Better to focus on the road that went directly to my career.

Then again, boys were sometimes cute. And funny. And nice. Like Micah…

"You're deep in thought," Foster said, though I hadn't even been aware of his presence in the room. "Are you brainstorming your future Pulitzer? Let me guess—*All Men Are Evil* by renowned überfeminist

Layney Logan."

I shucked my bag and jacket. "I'll be sure to give you credit for the title. Why are there so many folding chairs by the window?"

Foster snatched the coffee out of my hand. "Excellent. I needed a pick-me-up." He took the lid off while he continued. "The chairs apparently live in the newsroom now because Ms. Maple said they got some nicer ones from the school that closed. Also, I've lost control of the staff. They won't tell me what tonight's date is, only that I have to be here when you get your assignment." He took a swig. "What the hell is this?"

As he wiped the back of his hand across his lips, I answered, "It's a mocha."

"Since when do you drink that crap?"

Since never. "I just thought I would try something new. I'm all about stretching my comfort zone now, remember?" Grabbing the cup back from his hands, a little lukewarm java sloshed onto my hand. "There isn't anything wrong with sweet once in a while, right?"

His face screwed up into a look of confusion, but then he shrugged. "I guess not."

"I mean, I still like regular coffee, but a change from bitterness now and again is okay too, right?" My voice sounded unsure to my own ears.

"You're absolutely right, Logan. But I know you— you'll always go back to regular roast because sweet will bore you." He scrutinized me carefully. "You like a little bite."

"Sweet doesn't bore me."

"Whatever. It's coffee. It's not like you have to marry it."

I dared another sip, determined to give it a chance. I mean, why couldn't I like it? Just because I wasn't used to it didn't mean it wasn't good. I love chocolate. I'm obsessed with coffee. The color and foam were visually appealing and it smelled really good. On paper, we were a great match, café mochas and I.

Yet Foster laughed at my grimace as the cloying liquid went down the hatch.

I had two choices: persist and make myself miserable or admit that Foster was right. I hated giving him that little bit of satisfaction. What's worse, the fact that he had a foothold on my psyche appalled me.

I set the cup down and readied for battle.

"Ah. There goes the chin," Foster remarked. "Save the energy, Logan. We really don't need to pick this one apart. It's just coffee. If it makes you feel better, tomorrow I'll try a hazelnut latte or something."

Maryanne and Chelsea marched in looking apprehensive. Foster and I exchanged glances. The children were up to something. The silence thickened with tension and the girls nudged each other, hoping one would step up so the other wouldn't have to.

"Spill." The word barreled out of Foster, piercing the silence like a bullet.

Chelsea cleared her throat and looked at her shoes. "We are going to change things up a little this time and tell Layney who her date is now, when she gets her assignment."

"Okay," I said. That sounded good. Sometimes the not knowing made me edgy. "Who am I interviewing tonight?"

"Miles Bennington."

"Miles Bennington? The Wondertwin?"

Miles was one-half of a twin-set that refused to be separated. He and his sister, Ariana, were always together. Always. They weren't conjoined, but they may as well have been. That is why most kids called them "AirMiles."

"He agreed? I didn't think he went anywhere without his..."

Everyone looked at Foster. "He doesn't go anywhere without his sister," he deduced. "Which is why you guys kept me out of the loop, isn't it?"

Maryanne whispered, "It's a double date."

"No," Foster and I answered simultaneously.

"It's a perfect solution," Chelsea argued. "Jimmy will be there anyway, and after the last couple dates, we figured it might make you feel safer."

Sure, because double-dating with the devil is safe as houses.

"The whole point of this assignment is for Logan to get to know these guys and report back what girls are looking for when they date. If I'm there, the results would be skewed," Foster very thoughtfully added.

"Right," I said. "Wait, skewed how? What are you trying to say?"

He stepped back a little. "I just think my presence might distract you."

I narrowed my eyes and glared at him. "Why exactly do you think that?"

"We have a...history."

"Prehistoric."

"You might feel awkward."

"Why?"

"Because of your feelings—"

My hand covered his mouth. "Stop right there, asshat. I do not have *feelings* for you—at least none that don't include the desire for pinking shears." Foster winced, but I didn't stop. "I am a professional investigative reporter, and I don't let things like yesterday's garbage interfere with my ability to get the story." I turned to Chelsea and Maryanne. "If the only way to get Miles on this date is to take out AirMiles, we'll do what we have to do. But don't think we need to make it a double just because I've met a few bad apples. I don't need Foster's protection. I'm quite capable of handling myself." I held my hand out for the pink heart, not opening it as I put the cover back on my coffee and collected my things.

"Do you want me to pick you up?" Beelzebub asked.

I answered with an icy glare and formed my fingers into the shape of scissors snipping.

On my way out, I chucked the mocha into the wastebasket.

Tyler dangled the bag in front of me and I snatched it like a greedy kid from *Charlie and the Chocolate Factory*.

"Yay!" I tore into the bag and giggled at the picture on the mug. He'd painted a caricature of himself wearing a rhinestone Elvis jumpsuit holding hands with a caricature of me looking a lot closer to Kristen Bell than I usually do. "It's made of awesome."

"I'm glad you like it." He sat across from me. "So, excited about the double date tonight?"

I rolled my eyes. "I wouldn't have texted you about it if I thought you were going to mock me all day."

"Why do you hate Jimmy so much?" Tyler passed me a burger from the bag.

"Jimmy Foster? Because he's made it his life's purpose to annoy me. Why do you like him so much?"

Tyler shrugged. "I've had him in a few classes. He's always been nice."

"Bleh."

"So are you going to go out with Micah again?"

I stopped midbite. "Where did that come from?"

"He's been telling people he's hot for you."

"Get out."

"Whatever. I know you like him."

"Pass the ketchup. I don't dislike him. I'm not really in the market for a boyfriend."

He handed me a couple of packets of condiments. "If anyone should be in the market for a boyfriend, it should be you."

"You've been on one date with Stephanie, and now the whole world should be in love? Besides, I would make a terrible girlfriend."

Not that I wasn't happy that Tyler's date with this new Stephanie girl went well—I wanted him to be happy. Really I did. It's just that I'd just found him and I didn't want a girl to come between our budding friendship.

"Why do you say that? You'd be a great girlfriend if you just loosened up a little."

I sneered at him.

"Did you write down your dreams last night?"

"I couldn't remember any of them. It's like trying to hold on to a gust of wind."

Tyler sat back in his seat and watched me until I

77

GWEN HAYES

began fidgeting. I hate it when he does that. I know he has something to say. It's usually something I don't want to hear and usually something I need to.

"What already?"

"Do you think the dreams have something to do with your panic attack last week?"

"No." *Yes.* "Can I ask you a question?"

Tyler nodded.

"Whatever does a girl wear on a double date in hell?"

"I have no idea."

"Can I ask you another question?"

"Do I have a choice?"

"Not really. Will you go to the mall with me after school?"

Luckily, the helldate was a pizza joint and not too formal, so I stuck with jeans but added a really cute top I'd splurged on at Hollister because Tyler said it made my "eyes look greener" and "can we please go now?" I'm usually more of a t-shirt girl, but I needed a little confidence tonight. Foster would be looking for chinks in my armor—any perceived weakness, and I'd be toast.

AirMiles were already there with Foster, so I got to make an entrance. Which, of course, I love. Not. They were seated smack-dab in the middle of the room—which I hated—at a table for four. Ariana sat next to her brother and across from Foster. Which meant I got to sit right next to him.

Both guys stood up when I got to the table. Foster introduced me even though I'd known Miles for years. Puzzled by his odd behavior, I watched as his face flushed briefly. He was nervous too?

After the pizza got ordered, Foster tried to engage Ariana in conversation, presumably so I could get to know Miles. I say presumably because his effort went unnoticed by brother and sister, who couldn't seem to function in conversation unless they were finishing each other's sentences.

"Miles, you're in band still aren't you? Drums, right?" I asked.

"He is," answered Ariana. "He's so awesome. He also plays in a rock band called the Riff."

"The Riff," Miles repeated.

"I've heard of you guys," I answered. "You played at the park on the Fourth of July, right?"

"They did. Did you buy a CD?" she answered again.

"We were selling CDs at the show," Miles added.

I nudged Foster. "No...but I thought the band was great."

"Ariana," Foster began. "What do you like to do?"

"I'm in marching band too. But not the Riff."

"She's our manager," said Miles.

Ariana nodded. "I'm their manager."

Miles was cute—Ariana was cuter. It was a shame that it was only together that they possessed one personality.

After a little more chitchat, Ariana announced, "The Riff is playing at Lauren Parker's birthday bash next month."

A red haze clouded my vision at not only the name but the event. I'd spent most of my high school years pretending Lauren Parker didn't exist. Her little birthday bashes were the big highlight to a lot of students' years.

I hadn't been invited to one since the eighth grade.

The ice water in front of me saved me from a direct or immediate answer to that, and while I sipped, Foster said, "That's great, Miles. Lauren's parties are epic."

"You would know," I answered.

"Put your claws away, kitten," Foster mumbled to me, which only ratcheted up my anger—which I'm sure was his goal. "Your band will be great," he said to Miles. "Will you be there too? As the manager?" he asked Ariana.

"Oh yeah, I wouldn't miss it. It's the best party of the year."

"See, that's what I like to see," Foster answered. "People making the most of their high school years. Going to parties and sporting events and having fun."

"That's just like you to change the subject just so you can get another dig in."

"I'm not digging. Maybe you are just sensitive because you are the oldest teenager ever."

"Just because I don't go to parties or dances or dates doesn't mean I'm not getting the most of my high school experience." He was so infuriating. "For me, the most is preparing for college."

"And college will prepare you for a career, and a career will prepare you for retirement. Then what? Retirement will prepare you for death? When do you actually plan on living?"

The waitress set down our pizza, so I waited until she moved on before replying. "I happen to like my life. Just because I don't want to go drinking and partying doesn't mean I'm not living."

"No," he replied. "But not having any fun at all means you're not living."

"You just want to go to the party because you know there's always a sure thing there for you." I looked at Miles. "Lauren Parker's birthday bashes have been very good to Foster. In fact, I bet he's not the only one. I bet lots of guys cheat on their girlfriends at Lauren Parker's parties."

"This is not the time or the place, Layney," Foster reminded me.

"No, apparently, Lauren's rec room is the place."

"I knew you weren't over it." He put his pizza down. "Four years and I'm still hearing about one stupid night."

"This is the first time I've said anything since the eighth grade." Instead of putting my pizza down, I took a huge bite.

"You may not mention that night, but you refer to it with every snide remark and every distrustful glance."

"I see. So I should just completely trust the judgment of someone who thinks it's okay to cheat."

"I did not cheat on you."

I threw my piece onto my plate. "You made out with Lauren Parker at her fourteenth birthday party." I faced our dates again, who sat wide-eyed and stupefied. "He totally made out with Lauren Parker."

Foster's fingers clenched into a fist before he let out a deep, exasperated breath. "I didn't make out with her. I kissed her. Briefly."

"Oh please."

"It was spin the bottle," he explained to AirMiles. "It lasted maybe ten seconds."

"You had no business playing spin the bottle at a party that your girlfriend didn't attend."

"You were *supposed* to be there. You picked a fight

81

with me and then didn't show up."

"Oh, right. My bad. Then you totally had every right to kiss someone else."

"Gah." He raked his fingers through his hair. How they didn't get stuck in the gel is a mystery. "I wasn't even playing. They asked me to join and I said no. About fifteen minutes later, I realized I was having a terrible time, so I went to say goodbye to Mitch. I crouched down to tell him I was leaving, and the bottle stopped and pointed at me."

"So you had no choice but to make out with the birthday girl."

"I didn't make out with her. God, you're stubborn. Maybe I should have protested more, but jeez, Layney, I was thirteen. There was a lot of pressure. Everyone was looking at me, and I was still mad at you, and I didn't know what the right thing to do was. So, yes, I kissed her. Briefly. And then I left."

This really wasn't the time or the place, but that didn't seem to matter. "So that's your excuse, then? You were mad and people were looking at you? That's all it took to throw away what I thought was a good relationship?"

"You threw it away, not me."

"I didn't kiss anyone. I didn't bring anyone else into the mix."

"You were the one who brought her into it, not me. It was a dumb kiss during a dumb game of spin the bottle. If our relationship was so good, you would have laughed it off. But no, you were looking for a reason to break up."

"Well thank you so much for giving me such a good one, then."

"Don't mention it."

"Believe me, this is the last time I hope to ever talk about it. And Foster?"

"Yeah?"

"Where are our dates?"

At some point during our tirade, they must have taken off—undetected by the two top investigative journalists of our school. We waited another ten minutes just to be sure they didn't go to the restroom (and that gave me the willies thinking they went together) and we left too.

I felt sick and full of anger and maybe something close to regret.

Foster may have come closer to the truth than I cared to admit. Maybe I had been looking for a reason to break up. One that was easier for me to accept than I was just scared.

And one that didn't include the truth, the whole truth, and nothing but the truth.

8 CHAPTER EIGHT

Mr. July

Sk8erboy92: *What are you wearing right now?*

I smiled at my monitor.

LoisLayney: *A coat made from the fur of one hundred and one puppies. At least that is what the reporter whose column I'm editing probably thinks.*
Sk8erboy92: *Fine. What are you wearing under the coat, then?*

Micah made me laugh.

LoisLayney: *What are you doing?*
Sk8erboy92: *I'm standing on the street corner texting you IMs*

I JUMPED up and ran to my window. Sure enough, two houses down and under the streetlight, a boy in a hooded sweatshirt waved to me, the light glinting off the studs on his belt.

I punched his digits into my cell.

He answered with, "You don't look like you're wearing a fur coat."

"Why are you skulking around my street, skaterboy?"

"I was kinda hoping you'd come out and play with me."

My toes curled into the carpet. "I'm pretty sure my parents would object. It's a school night, you know."

"Just for a little while?"

I hadn't sneaked out of the house since…well, since I used to swap spit with Foster. And even then, we didn't usually get too physical when we were on our forbidden dates. Neither one of us had been ready to test our boundaries yet. We saved that kind of stuff for stolen moments when our parents knew where we were. Safer. No getting carried away.

I'm not sure if Micah worried about getting carried away.

"Micah…"

"I just want to talk. I promise. I'll keep my hands in my pockets the whole time."

The clock read after midnight. My parents turned in at 10:30 sharp and slept like the dead.

"I'll be down in a few."

A bitter wind bit at my face as I got closer to the corner. Maybe it would have been more of a brisk or energizing wind to me if I really wanted to be out there. But that was my problem. I didn't want to be out there. Out in the dating world. I hadn't since Foster, and knowing that made me angry that I'd cloistered myself away like a nun all these years.

So, I was going to take a walk with a hot boy who liked me. Whether I wanted to or not.

Micah tentatively reached for my hand. His was warm, comforting, and despite my misgivings, gave me a slight thrum of excitement in my belly.

"How many more dates do you still have to go on?" he asked as we began walking, hand in hand down my street.

"Six." I shuddered from disgust as much as from the chilly wind. "I don't think I can do it."

"Sure you can."

"It seems to me you should be trying to help me get out of them."

"Nah. I'm not worried about the competition. The more of them you date, the more you'll like me. It's Jimmy Foster I wonder about."

"Foster? Why?"

"No reason. Are you cold?"

He started to take off his jacket, but I stopped him. "No, don't. I'm okay. Why are you wondering about Foster?"

A rock under his shoe suddenly became very interesting, and we came to a stop as he toed it back and forth. "It's just that he comes up a lot."

"You mean when you ask me about my day and I tell you it sucked so you ask why and he's always the reason?"

"It's just…nothing. It's dumb." He started walking again, but there was some really huge, big, dumb, ugly elephant in front of us that we pretended wasn't.

"This walk isn't going the way you planned, is it?"

Micah smirked and squeezed my hand. "Not exactly." He stopped again and reached for my other hand. "It's no secret that I really like you, right?"

He played with my fingers so he wouldn't have to look into my eyes, I think. How reassuring that even a guy like Micah had reservations about his prowess sometimes.

But I wasn't sure I was the best candidate to restore his confidence either. "It's no secret that I'm really a sandwich short of a picnic when it comes to feelings and emotions and…stuff, right?"

He puckered his lips into a wry little smile. "I'd like to go on a real date when you are done with the undates. Is that even remotely likely?"

I wanted to reassure him. I wished I was the girl who could smile and bat her eyelashes and say just the right coy thing to make him glad he expended the effort to spend time with me.

Micah looked so handsome in the moonlight. Nothing was stopping me from wrapping my arms around his neck and kissing him. He'd be a great kisser. He'd be a good boyfriend. Nothing was stopping me except the heavy weight of an anvil pressing on my chest.

Speak, Layney. "If I said it's not out of the realm of possibilities, would that be enough for you? At least for tonight?"

"Sure."

Sure.

We resumed walking, me holding my arms tightly across my chest. What was wrong with me? Who replaced my blood with ice water? A dozen times I tried to make something light and witty come out of my mouth, but there was nothing I could think of to say. I don't really know why I could feel so attracted to Micah, but at the same time, that attraction made me feel claustrophobic.

There must be something I could say to lighten the mood. "I'm not normal, Micah."

So much for light and witty.

"What are you talking about?"

"I really like you too. I do, I swear. It's just…it's like…"

"Relax." He ruffled my hair. "I'm not going anywhere."

"Why?" Not that I wasn't glad. I just didn't understand why he'd want to hang around.

"I can see you have issues. I'm not sure even you know what they are. But I'm not the kind of guy who drops out of a race because I see a hill. Challenges turn me on." From the corner of my eye, I watched him form his next sentence as if a thought was just dawning on him. "I think you're worth it, Layney."

He kissed my hand when he delivered me safely to my door.

I think my blood was defrosting.

"If you plan to be alive to walk at graduation, James Theodore Foster, you will fix this now." I thrust the dreaded pink invitation in his face and didn't bother to try to hide the sheer terror shining in my eyes. Let him see my weakness.

He unballed the paper and started laughing hysterically.

"There is nothing funny about this situation. And you won't be laughing when you're dead. Fix this."

"They set you up for karaoke? This is priceless. God, I can't wait."

"No no no!" The line is drawn. I refuse. I am not singing karaoke. Call your staff. The story is dead."

I stormed away but he caught me at the door. "Now, just wait. The story is not dead. We can find a compromise."

"There is not a compromise in the universe that will get me on a stage to sing. Not happening. I'm tired of being in the center ring of your circus, Foster."

He squared my shoulders with his hands. "The staff chose the venue. I swear I didn't set this one up."

I closed my eyes, suddenly very tired. "Maybe not this date, but all of this is your doing. I'm not sure why you felt the need to manipulate me with all these games, but it stops now. I'm done."

"Layney."

I opened my eyes.

"You're overreacting. I know you weren't completely on board with this story, but you would never have agreed if you didn't feel it had some merit."

Something clicked inside, or more like clunked, and I slumped over, hanging my head between us. "It wasn't supposed to be like this. This was supposed to be the best year ever. I don't know if we can pull this off anymore."

"Whoa," he replied, succinct yet full of wonder. "Um. Are we still talking about karaoke?"

I lifted my head and squinted at him. "I'm not doing it. And I'm not doing this stupid story, and I don't think I'm doing this stupid paper either."

Cupping my chin with one hand, he nodded my head for me while he said, "Yes you will."

We stood too close. I could see the flecks of color, golds and greens in his eyes, and I was sure he saw the unshed tears caught in mine. The moment bore down on us, heavy, like the feel of the air right before a thunderstorm. A little sigh escaped my lungs, and my chin tilted just a bit. His palm smoothed a small path from my chin to my cheek, and his fingers feathered into my hairline. We were powerless to stop, and our lips inched closer.

Closer.

The first brief pass of his mouth shocked me even though I had known it was coming. I clutched his arms for support and kept my eyes open. He hesitated, his forehead wrinkled in bewilderment, and then he swooped in again, both hands in my hair, and the bottom of my world dropped away.

We kissed with the same parry and thrust that we did everything. An answer to a taunt. Vying for what seemed to be the same thing, the clash of wills and lips.

I'd never kissed anyone I despised before. Madness. Nothing else could describe it. Neither one of us wanted to be kissing the other, yet I don't think any amount of force on Earth could have pulled me away from him just then.

I hated him for making me want to kiss him. If we had been any two other people, the kissing might have put a cease-fire on the war. Instead, our lip lock incensed us further. Four years of hurt feelings and bruised egos met with a longing we'd both done our best to deny. It wasn't pretty. Movie kisses never looked like this felt.

He rubbed my heart raw.

The bell rang, and we stumbled away from each other, reeling as if we'd just gotten off a carnival ride. I resisted the urge to touch my mouth, though it felt bruised and swollen. I blinked several times, but the room seemed slow to right itself.

Foster cleared his throat and rubbed the back of his neck absently. "I guess we'll figure out a different venue for tonight's date, and I'll get back to you. I know you're scared of singing in public."

Wait a minute. "I'm not scared. I just don't like to." With ever fiber of my being.

"Right."

"I'm not scared."

"I just agreed with you."

"No, you didn't."

"I said 'right.'"

"But you didn't mean 'right.' You meant 'sure' in a patronizing way."

"This is the most ridiculous argument ever."

"We aren't arguing," I said, even though it sounded ridiculous to me too.

"For Christ's sake. I'll fix it so you don't have to sing karaoke, okay?"

"Don't do me any favors, Foster. I'll do the stupid karaoke date. I'm not scared of singing or dating." As I turned heel and fled the room, I realized I was pretty much my own worst enemy.

I really hated Foster.

Wanting to crawl out of my skin, I clutched my microphone in a death grip. He was out there somewhere, watching. I just couldn't see him. Thankfully, I couldn't see anyone. A sea of black— either that or I was unconscious. Which was preferable to standing on stage waiting to humiliate myself.

Interspersed with the nausea and feelings of rage, there was also an aberrant thought tickling my mind. All evening, when I least expected to, *bam! I kissed Foster today*. Okay, at first it was *Foster kissed me today*. But I participated in the kissing, and what's more, it was good kissing, in an oddly ugly way. I simultaneously wanted to do it again and wash my mouth out with soap.

Of course, if I killed him, I could just choose the soap and get over it.

Mr. July stood next to me. Ben Something-or-Other. I know, bad reporter. I just couldn't be bothered with facts just then. He was nice, I think. Polite anyway, but the night had been out of control for me since before I got there. I tried to respond to his small talk, but knowing I had to sing before the hour was done wigged me out. He probably thought I had a problem with crack. I emptied all the sugars into my water glass so I could make a chain with the empty wrappers. I picked at invisible fuzz on my shirt. I rambled about how much I love journalism. Basically, I was a big, fat mess.

Which lead to the magic moment—sharing the stage with my new guy, getting ready to sing "Can You Feel the Love Tonight?" Except that the DJ dude put "Hakuna Matata" on by accident, so we had to wait for a minute while he figured out which track our song was. I actually would have preferred to sing the mistake just to get off the stage faster.

I hate Foster.

"Yeah, you've said that a couple times already," Ben said.

I didn't realize I had said it out loud. "Sorry."

"It's okay. I have a surprise for you after we're

done."

I couldn't get a question off before the music started. If anything good could be said about the song it would be that I knew all the words. I'd watched the movie a bajillion and seven times. And then Ben surprised me by turning into a complete cornball.

He was magnificent. I tried to keep up, but it was hard over the giggling. Right before my eyes, Ben Something-or-Other turned into an aging Vegas act. Winking at the ladies, hamming up the lyrics—all he needed was a powder blue leisure suit. All the pressure was taken off me and I actually enjoyed myself. I sang along, though not loudly, whenever I was able to get my laughter under control.

The audience ate him up like ice cream. He swaggered and waggled his eyebrows. He pulled out a bunch of *American Idol* moves, closing his eyes, reaching for the sky. The girls all played along, wolf whistling and blowing kisses. At one point, they were all standing, waving their arms above their heads to the music.

Near the end of the song, he reached for my hand and placed it on his heart, serenading me. He even winked at me right before the crowd went crazy with the hooting and hollering.

I thought that was my surprise. That he threw himself under the bus to save my dignity. It would have been enough, Lord knew. I owed him my firstborn already. But no, Ben S. had something else up his sleeve. Something so potent that if he ever decided to use his powers for evil, we were all doomed.

Ben slipped the DJ a bill—I couldn't see the denomination. As we exited the stage, the DJ called out the next act, "Is there a Jimmy Foster in the house? Jimmy, we're ready for your number."

Foster poked his head out of the swinging door to the kitchen and then tried to duck back inside.

"There he is," said Ben, pointing so that all eyes in "the house" turned his way.

All we could see were his shoes. They turned slowly and a hand clasped the top of the door and pushed it open agonizingly slow. He stood for a second, looking to me like he might bolt, but then a spotlight found him and he surrendered. Foster walked his green mile to the stage, questioning me as he passed us.

I shrugged. I really didn't know.

The DJ handed him a mic, pointed to the screen, and started the music. Foster glared at me, but not a thing in the world could have wiped the smile off my face.

Because few things were funnier than watching James Theodore Foster sing "Like a Virgin" at Shel's Coffee and Karaoke Klatch.

9 CHAPTER NINE

Mr. August

LOOKING back, I didn't know what "lily-livered" meant, exactly, but I heard it in a cartoon once, and that was exactly what I was. As in lily-livered, spineless coward hiding behind the door of the girls' room because I knew Foster was standing outside of it. I hadn't been alone with him in two days. Since all the kissing.

I checked my watch. Shit, I was going to be late for class. What was he doing out there? I cracked the door again. He was still standing with his back against the lockers. The hall emptied of all but a few students. Shit, shit, shit.

I paced the worn linoleum. The windows were specifically designed to keep students in, so there was no help there. Not that I was desperate. Who was I kidding? I would gladly have jumped out a window to avoid being alone with Foster right then. Even if the windows were on the second floor.

The door opened so I ducked into a stall. My jittery fingers had trouble with the lock, and the door pushed against me.

I pushed back. "Occupied." God, it wasn't like there weren't three other stalls.

"Then unoccupy it or I'm coming in with you."

"Foster?" *You have got to be kidding me.* "This is the girls' room. You can't be in here."

"You haven't given me much choice, Logan."

"Go away."

"No. Come out."

"No."

He gave a big shove just as I was letting go, and the door smacked me in the nose.

"Crap!"

He barged in behind the door. "Oh God. I'm so sorry. I didn't do that on purpose. You know that, right? Are you okay?" His voice sounded tinny and far away. And getting further.

No words would form. All I could do was moan and hold my face as I leaned against the stall. I squinted against the flashing lights that were probably only in my head but hurt my eyes just the same. I was afraid I was going to throw up, and I wasn't sure, exactly, which direction the toilet was.

"You're bleeding."

Foster steadied me and then pulled me out of the stall and to the sinks. He plopped me up onto the counter like I weighed nothing. Which would have seemed kind of manly if I hadn't already been on the receiving end of his testosterone driven door push. And if the counter hadn't been full of standing water and soggy paper towels.

I wouldn't let him pull my hands away from my

nose. "It hurts," I whined.

"I know, I know. I'm so sorry. I just want to see it."

I dropped my hands, and he tipped my head back. "Crap."

"What is it?"

"You're a mess." He wet some fresh paper towels and held them directly on my nose. "Seriously. You are a mess."

"It's your fault. You did this to me."

His eyes widened, and I felt like I should say something more to clarify. Because all of the sudden, it wasn't just my bloody nose that we were talking— or not talking—about. And while I'd justifiably blamed him for everything all those years, it felt kind of shitty to tell him that while he was trying to be nice.

"I never wanted you to get hurt."

"I know."

He pulled away the towel, grimaced, and promptly put it back. "I think we need to get the nurse."

"She's only here on Wednesdays."

"What? Why?"

"Budget cutbacks."

"But people don't only get hurt on Wednesdays. That's so stupid."

I shrugged. "You wouldn't believe how many girls get cramps only on Wednesdays now, though."

He looked puzzled.

"So they can go home early." His expression didn't change. "Never mind."

"Keep your chin tilted up." He started wiping up my face. "Why have you been avoiding me?"

"I haven't."

He stopped wiping and shot me a look of disbelief.

"Okay. Maybe I've been a little unavailable. I just…" What? What was I just? "I guess I just didn't want to talk about…you know."

"Well we can't pretend it didn't happen."

"Why not?"

"Because it did happen. And it could happen again."

"It could?"

"Sure. And we'll never know when. We'll be going about our business and all of the sudden we'll be kissing."

"We will?"

"And all because we never talked about it."

"So you are trying to tell me that if we don't talk about it, then it will happen again." Maybe I could just transfer schools instead.

"Yeah. Except it will probably happen again even if we do talk about it."

"But why?"

He stopped mopping my face and leaned in very close. "Because it didn't suck. If it had sucked, we could have the 'let's never talk about that again' conversation and be done with it. You stopped bleeding, by the way."

Why do people always think talking about things makes them better? I didn't subscribe to that channel. "Why do we have to have any conversation about it at all?"

"We don't. But be prepared for the consequences."

"But you said that we'd kiss again either way, so why do we have to talk about it?"

"You're right. We don't. We can just get straight to

the action if you want."

I never felt less like kissing anyone than I did as I sat there on a counter in the girls' bathroom surrounded by bloody paper towels, my nose throbbing, and my ass in a puddle of what I hoped was water.

And then he kissed me.

His mouth slanted over mine and I wrapped my arms around his neck. Some protest, huh? Foster splayed his hands on my hips, and my knees made room for him to lean in closer, and he couldn't get close enough if you had asked me.

The anger was missing this time. The change was subtle because we still weren't kissing in the Hilary Duff/Chad Michael Murray at the end of a Disney movie kind of way. The intensity hadn't lessened, just the fury.

And passion filled the vacuum the anger had created. The bitterness I knew a thing or two about. This passion stuff sneaked up on me. It was as if I wanted to take from him and give to him at the same time—and like my body was so happy to finally circumvent my brain that it unleashed all the hormones I'd kept at bay all these teen years.

My legs crossed behind him, pulling him toward me, and he groaned, a sound that reverberated in my veins like a choir during a crescendo. Shamelessly, I tugged and pulled at him, forcing his fingers to dig into my hips harder and mercilessly.

I angled to the right at the same time he angled to his left, and we bumped noses, setting fire to my sore one. I gasped and pulled back.

"Shit!" Stars, stars, everywhere I looked, stars. I covered my poor schnoz with my hands.

"Oh God, not again. I'm really sorry, Layney."

"It's okay." I said through my hands. "I probably deserve to get smacked in the face every time I kiss you."

He pried my fingers away from my nose. "Oh jeez. I think we really should go find out where the nurse is the other four days of the week."

"Is it bleeding again?"

"A little. And, um, your eyes are looking a little…swollen. And somewhat discolored."

"Are you freaking kidding me? You gave me a black eye?"

"No…I think I gave you two black eyes. I'm really, really sorry."

An errant, vain thought flitted through my head—I didn't want him to see me with two black eyes. I wanted him to see me…pretty.

Stop it, Layney.

I tentatively touched my nose. What if it was broken? "I knew you were evil. I didn't realize you were physically dangerous too."

He winced. "Seriously. We should go get you checked out."

"Nobody is going to believe I got hit with a door. I don't even want to know what the rumor mill is going to churn out."

"Layney, I'm not kidding. That color under your eyes isn't one you see in a rainbow. It's not natural."

He took a step back and I slid off my perch. Only the rest of the room kind of slid with me, and I slumped against Foster.

"God. I am the worst kind of ass," he said as he picked me up and carried me toward the door. "Your butt is wet."

"I know. You sat me down in a puddle. Foster, don't I have a date tonight?"

I did have a date that night.

And the preparations were not going well at all.

"Can't you do your own makeup?" Tyler asked me with a makeup sponge in one hand and a jar of cover-up in the other.

"You're supposed to be my best friend."

"Yeah, sure. But I don't know how to do this stuff."

"The makeup was your idea."

"All I said was that they used stage makeup when I was in the all-school play last year, and that it covered Tommy's black eye. I didn't say I knew how to apply it."

I suppose we looked ridiculous. I'll give my mom credit—she didn't bat an eye when she found me and the Hawaiian in her bedroom using her vanity table. I think she was just glad I had a friend finally. She worried.

Tyler set the jar down. "I need to watch ESPN or something. I'm feeling all weird."

"I promise you won't turn into a girl by holding a makeup sponge for too long."

Ty didn't answer and instead he sat on my parents' bed behind me. "Are you sure it was just a door, Layney?"

Our eyes met in the mirror. "I promise it was just a door."

"You know if anyone ever tries to hurt you, I'm your guy, right?"

A smile stretched across my face and my heart

swelled with genuine love for my BFF. "I know."

And I did know. Okay, so he wasn't so good at shopping or date preparation. And yeah, he actually thought a French manicure had something to do with tongue. But he was mine. I trusted Tyler the instant I met him. We were meant to be friends.

So it sort of slipped out, "I made out with Logan after he beamed me with the door in the girls' bathroom today."

"You're joking, right?"

I shook my head.

"What happened to 'Jimmy Foster is the spawn of Satan'?"

I shrugged. "I think it's a hex. Someone in our school has been practicing the dark arts or something."

Tyler scratched his head. He was either wondering what was wrong with me or how he ended up with the dubious position of riding shotgun in my life. "What did Jimmy say?"

"About what?"

"About making out."

"He didn't say anything. So this makeup is making me look kind of orange. Kind of like a bruised orange, actually."

"Am I hearing this right? You guys kissed in the girls' bathroom for the first time since middle school and neither of you said anything?"

I spun the stool slowly to face him, shooting him really big, really fake smile. "It was sort of the second time since middle school. We might have kissed for a minute the other day before the karaoke date."

"Oh you might have, huh?"

"It happened very fast, but that was the impression

that I got."

"Layney, I love you, kiddo. But you are one messed-up little girl."

"I know. I don't even like him."

"So you kissed him because..."

"I was hoping you would be smarter about this kind of stuff and maybe you could tell me."

"I am smarter than you, that's true. And the reason you kissed him is because you still have feelings for him."

"Don't be stupid."

Tyler tossed one of my mother's pillows at me. "You look like you spend every day fake-n-baking at the tanning salon. Who is your date tonight?"

"I don't know yet. I don't have feelings for Foster, either. Other than feelings of revulsion and repulsion."

"What about Micah?"

"What about Micah?" I turned back to the mirror and used Mom's cold cream to get the dayglow off my face.

"Do you like them both?"

"I don't like either of them that way."

"Right."

"Can we not do this now? I look like a poster for domestic violence awareness."

And I felt battered on the inside too. Did I like them both? Did that make me a bad person? One of them was bad for me, and I didn't trust him. The other was probably perfect for me—I really didn't trust him either.

An hour later, Tyler dropped me off at Hootenanny's, our small town answer to T.G.I.Fridays. On the way, we had picked up a pair of those ridiculously large sunglasses that Paris Hilton wears. They did the trick, but Hootenanny's wasn't brightly lit by any means. I bumped into the hostess podium and a table on the way to meet my date.

He stood when I arrived—score one for Mr. August. "I'm Jake Faraday."

"Hi Jake, I'm Layney Logan."

Jake was cute. I think. Hard to say in the dark.

"I'm sorry," he began. "But your sunglasses are still...um...on. In case you forgot or something."

"Yeah. I know. I just came from the optometrist. My pupils are dilated. I'm very sensitive."

"Okay." He smiled.

I think.

The waitress brought us the special desert the staff had preordered for us—a huge hot fudge sundae for two, with whipped cream and cherries on top. At the risk of sounding like a girl, a dose of chocolate went a long way in soothing the rotten—not to mention confusing—day I'd been through.

"So, Jake, tell me about yourself."

"I'm a junior. I don't have a girlfriend...but I'm looking for one. And I'm on the cheer squad."

The spoon of ice cream stopped short of my mouth. "You're a cheerleader?" I blurted.

"Yes. And I'm straight. Just to be clear."

"I would never have...okay, you're right. I probably would have."

"It's okay. Most people do. But cheering isn't just for gay guys anymore. In fact most are really there to score with the hot girls."

"Um, oh."

Jake had this strange way of punctuating the end of his sentences—like it was the last word of a cheer.

He startled me several times and drew attention to our table. I wanted to wave to people. *Hey, look, it's Too Loud Guy and his legally blind, blind date.*

"Actually, the first cheerleaders were all men. Did you know that?"

"I had no idea."

"The first squad was from the University of Minnesota. They were called yell leaders."

"Well, okay."

"Females didn't start participating until 1923."

"Wow, you sure know your cheer history."

"It's my ticket out of this town."

Jake then proceeded to fill me in on every detail I never needed to know about cheerleading. Including the difference between a Herkie and a hurdler, the correct spelling of pompon, and that he was hoping to get a full-ride scholarship to the state college after competitions next year.

My general disdain for the girls who wore the short, pleated skirts might have lessened a little when I heard how long their practices were every single day. Yeah, a lot of them were snotty and were granted privileges because they were pretty or rich—but it sounded like they also worked really hard. And I respected that. I just wished sometimes they would work a little harder on being less stuck-up.

Jake got louder and louder until I decided I was really glad I was wearing the anonymous dark shades. The further I shrank into the corner of my booth seat, the more gregarious he became. He was nice, really nice. He was just very…excited about his future.

"So, Jake. What do you want to do after college?"

"I'm hoping to get my Master of Library Science."

A librarian? Mr. Herkie wanted to be a librarian. Once again, the sunglasses shielded my date from my incredulous eyes. I guess, in a strange way, Foster did me a favor by trying to break my nose.

"What about you? What do you want to do after college?" he asked before he shoveled another bite, totally encroaching the boundary between our separate scoops.

I sat back, miffed about the sundae poaching. Clearly I wouldn't be giving Jake Farraday a rose at the end of this date. "An investigative reporter."

"Like newspapers?"

"They are my first choice."

He didn't notice I had stopped eating. "Aren't they, like, dying? I mean, not just the local paper. Aren't a bunch of them going bankrupt?"

He would have ducked if he could see the überglare I shot him. Then again, he wasn't wrong.

"You don't really have that TV reporter vibe either."

While I didn't want to be a glossy newscaster sitting behind a desk on Channel 4, I could totally pull off live reporting in a war zone or an interview with the president. Better than Mr. Too Loud could pull off shushing someone in the stacks.

Jake started talking about cheers again, and I tried to de-bitter my mood. It wasn't his fault that the industry was changing. Sure, he could have been a little more tactful about my lack of television-worthy attributes—but he was only the messenger. Too many things were changing this year—the roadmap I'd worked on so hard the last four years was becoming riddled with detours.

I realized, too late, that I had been tuning Jake out

and he was waiting for a response. So I nodded.

Big mistake.

He popped out of his seat. "Great. I won't be as loud as I would during a game, since we are inside." He readied himself, rolling his head and shrugging, and then took a deep breath. "Ready? O-KAY!"

O-GOD! Not ready. Not ready.

What had I agreed to? I recalled something about a cheer he had written. Did I want to hear it? I looked around the dining room hoping someone else would stop him. He had their attention—but nobody made any moves to interfere.

As he showed me the moves he choreographed to the words he had written, I wondered where Foster was hiding and if he thought this was hilarious or not. Maybe he still felt really bad about blackening my eyes. Maybe his stomach did little flips every time he remembered how my mouth felt under his. Maybe he was just as confused as I was.

But maybe I really did deserve to get smacked in the face every time I kissed him.

10 CHAPTER TEN

Mr. September

" I 'D like to make it clear from the start that I am gay, gay, gay. Like, when I come out of the closet, I'm usually wearing my sister's prom dress kind of gay."

I looked at Mr. September across the bench and said the first thing that came to mind. "God, you're so lucky."

He blinked several times, not sure what to make of me. "I am?"

"Do you know how many times I wished I were gay? Of course, knowing my luck I wouldn't understand girls any better than I do boys, but still."

Mr. September, aka Morgan Harris, and I were enjoying an autumn afternoon at the pumpkin patch. We'd each gotten a hot cider and settled in for the getting-to-know-you portion of the date when he blurted out his sexual orientation.

He sipped his cider, regarding me closely over the

lip of the cup. "Boys are supposedly easier, but I'm not sure I buy that either. Of course, I don't date high school boys."

I turned toward him. "Me either!" He cocked his head a little. "I mean usually. Before this calendar thing, I didn't date. I consider these interviews anyway."

The rigidness in his spine loosened as he exhaled. "I was really worried about this date. I'm not exactly hiding in a closet, but I don't usually make announcements about my queerness either. There just aren't a lot of photogenic alternatives for your calendar on the math team. I'm sort of…it."

He wasn't joking. I'd seen the math team. They were most likely the future generation of the most important and influential people on the planet (think Bill Gates), but they weren't the easiest to look at. Columbia High School, fifteen miles away, was the opposite. If I were to voluntarily date high school boys, I would have started in their campus math labs.

I patted his arm. "Don't feel bad. I worry about every date. Not to weird you out or anything, but you should know that my co-editor is hiding behind one of the scarecrows, watching our every move."

Morgan jerked his head sideways, trying to see behind anything tall enough for someone to spy from. "Is he cute?"

"He's not without visual appeal," was the least incriminating thing I could think of to say.

Morgan and I finished the ciders and walked around the farm, stopping at the petting zoo for a few minutes of quality time with really cute baby animals and a lot of kids with runny noses. He told me about the college guy he met last weekend that he hoped would be his boyfriend soon.

"How do you know, though?" I asked.

"I don't understand the question."

We were heading toward the pumpkins, so I walked gingerly to avoid the mud. "How do you make the leap from 'I like looking at you' to 'I want to be your girlfriend'? I mean boyfriend, as the case may be. How do you know that *this* guy is the one for you and not *that* guy?"

"Oh that's easy. I usually assign each guy a destination."

"Are you speaking math? I don't understand you."

"Okay, pick one guy and tell me what locale in the world you think he best represents."

I picked up a perfectly round pumpkin and thought of Micah. "Someplace...warm. With tiki lights and drum music and sand."

"That pumpkin is too perfect," he answered. "You want one with a little character. Okay, now pick another guy and do the same thing."

I set the pumpkin down and thought about Foster. "Someplace noisy and confusing. With lots of different smells and bad weather and foul language. And a lot of energy. Like New York."

"Okay," Morgan handed me a strangely shaped pumpkin. "Now, where would you rather live?"

Paradise? Or the city? Sun soaked and mellow or messy and scary and dark and exciting and eclectic and...

"The city," I answered with a sigh. A big, heavy sigh. "And I'll take this strange, misshapen pumpkin too, I guess."

***

"Press Enter, Ms. Logan. You've done all the

damage you can do."

My hand shook, and every time I got near the keyboard, I pulled it way like I'd touched a hot burner. "I can't, Mr. Blake."

"We've gone over the layout several times. It looks great."

"What if there is something we both missed. Why isn't Foster here?"

The jerk scheduled a photo shoot when we were supposed to be sending the live version of the *Follower* into cyberspace. The first issue was hitting the stands, and he was MIA.

"Layney," he began sagely, as if he'd had to talk me off the ledge a hundred times in the last four years. Which he had, of course. The man had the patience of a saint. "The best part about a digital version is we can fix it instantly if we need to."

He was right. When we used to go to print, changes were impossible. This was progression, right?

I still wished Foster were there.

Ugh, did I really just think that?

"Jimmy already said he thought it looked great, but he wanted you to be the one to have the final say. So have your say, Ms. Logan."

The tone of Mr. Blake's words made me wonder what else he was really trying to say. Jimmy Foster wanted me to have the final say, so if it sucked, he could pass the blame to me. No big surprise.

I shot a covert glance over my shoulder. Mr. Blake had his arms crossed and he was studying me. He shook his head as if he could read my thoughts.

I suppose it was possible that Foster was attempting to be magnanimous. Unlikely but possible. But if he was giving me the upper hand for any reason other than to cover his own ass, I still suspected ulterior motives.

I clicked Send, and we were live.

I exhaled a breath I'd been holding since August.

We'd done it. It was a free blog still; the software we wanted was going to have to wait until we netted the results from the calendar. But the *Follower* still had a pulse.

We'd done it.

But I kind of missed the "we" part at the moment.

Still irrationally angry with Foster for deserting me at the launch, I threw my books into my locker. Before I could slam the door closed, a hand grabbed the edge of it. My girl parts recognized the scent of Micah's cologne instantly, and they reacted as can be expected from parts behaving autonomously from the brain they are supposedly attached to.

I turned into the cage of his body and sighed. "Hey."

"Hey yourself. I just wanted to remind you that in three dates' time, you should be prepared."

Did he absolutely have to smell so good? "Prepared for what, exactly?"

"Intense wooage."

"Is wooage a word?" I leaned into the locker next to mine.

"It should be if it isn't."

"Micah, I'm just not sure about this. I haven't exactly relaxed my position on dating, despite having been on nine of them. Probably because I've been on nine of them."

He fingered a lock of hair on my cheek while

closing my locker with his right hand. "I never doubted you would be a challenge."

We both sensed our non-aloneness at the same time. Three feet away, Foster had rooted himself to the floor, his face a stern mask of fortunately unreadable emotions.

"Hey," I offered, feeling foolish and indignant that I felt that way. I wasn't doing anything wrong. It's not like I had a boyfriend. I hadn't been seeking Micah out. I didn't know he was going to find me and flirt with me at my locker.

Yet I still felt like crap.

Micah dropped his hand, lingering slower than the situation called for. "I'll talk to you later, Lois Layney."

I nodded without making eye contact. My lips drew in tightly, like I was afraid he was going to swoop in and lay one on me.

Even after he'd left, Micah's presence remained.

Foster just stood there. I finally gave in and looked at him, immediately wishing I'd left when Micah had. Foster's expression matched my memory of the day we'd broken up—a little disbelief with a slightly angry chaser.

"Are you dating him now?"

"No." Pushing off the lockers, steam gathered in my head where good sense should have been instead. "It's none of your business." I slammed the locker closed.

"None of my business?"

He reached for my shoulder, but I stepped out of his grip. "If I were seeing Micah, which I'm not, it would be none of your business."

"I think it very much is."

"Why?" I waved him off and started walking down the hall. "You know what, never mind. I don't really care."

"Why? I'll tell you why. Because," he blustered while catching up to me. "Because the contract, which you helped write, clearly states no physical contact. This is supposed to be about the story, not your personal life. You used to be more professional than this."

I froze in my tracks. "This has nothing to do with the story, Foster, and everything to do with you wanting to manipulate me. And…and that stupid kiss."

"Which one?"

"Both of them, okay? Neither of them should ever have happened. And now, because you pawed me in the girl's bathroom, you think you have a right to tell me who I can and can't date? It's not like you stepped up and professed your undying love for me." As the words tumbled out, I wanted to scoop them back in. "I'm not a pawn in your chess game. You do whatever it takes to keep me off balance and it isn't going to work anymore."

"Excuse me? I still have marks where you dug your shoes into my back."

The memory sent a rush of heat to my face. "This is stupid, Foster. I don't know why the kissing happened, but it needs to stop. And not because of Mr. March or you thinking you have some right to tell me how to live. It needs to stop because kissing you is destructive behavior."

"Do you think you are any better for me than I am for you? You drive me insane. You're the most annoying person I've ever met. Nothing I do is good enough for you and everything I say is exactly wrong." He raked his hands through his hair and started back down the hall.

This time I ran to catch up to him. "I drive you insane? At least I don't intentionally look for ways to set you up and humiliate you."

"Layney, you addressed me as Lucifer in AP English yesterday."

"It's not like that embarrassed you. You probably liked it. I don't purposely find things to make you self-conscious about the way you look."

He stopped and drew in a deep breath, but that little vein in his temple showed me he was anything but cool headed. "You and I both know I don't mean it when I tease you. I think it's been made a little more than obvious that despite my better judgment, you appeal to me physically."

"Oh, I'm touched." I covered my heart with my hand. "I appeal to you physically despite your better judgment. All these flowery words—what's a girl to do?"

"Flowery words?" It happened slowly, but Foster's face changed by degrees until he was someone I didn't recognize. His eyes darkened, his face grew taut, his jaw squared. I'd finally found the button.

Part of me wished maybe I hadn't pushed it.

The other part was some strange girl waking up and taking over my brain. She wanted him to bring it. The adrenaline rush skittered through my body. The hairs on my nape rose to the occasion. I inhaled sharply, the air sudden and swift, and I felt like I could shoot sparks from my fingertips.

"Flowery words?" he repeated.

I was so afraid he would ruin the moment with

something lame, like "I got your flowery words right here" that I closed the distance and latched onto Foster in a clinch that rivaled the covers of my mother's romance novels.

The bruising kiss tasted like anger and bad choices. And I couldn't get enough of it. His mouth crushed mine, stealing my breath and my wisdom while it consumed me like flames to paper. That strange girl who took over my brain? She reveled in the mess I was making.

He broke first, gasping for air like he'd just hit the surface after a tumble from the deck of a sinking ship. His hands still cupped my head and he pulled me into his chest, and I closed my eyes and allowed his heartbeat to soothe what I hadn't been able to unburden myself from. Not in a long time.

Foster stroked pacifying patterns on my back, giving us time to regroup, or in my case, reload.

I pushed away the way I'd pull off a Band-Aid. "Why?"

"I wish I knew."

"Maybe we just needed to get it out of our system?"

"I don't think kissing you will make it anything but harder. Feel free to notice the double entendre there at the end."

There was something really sexy about a guy who could speak to me in literary terms.

He exhaled harshly and bent his head, rubbing the tense muscles at the back of his neck. The impulse to place a soft kiss at the exposed skin rocked me. When had I become someone I didn't know or understand?

He finally spoke, and his words shifted the tectonic plates under my feet. "I haven't been able to get you out of my system in ten years."

Despite my heart slamming against my chest like a paddle ball, I teased him. "AP English but remedial math, huh? It may seem like ten years but—"

"It was a Wednesday." He raised his head and pinned me with a dark gaze.

"What was a Wednesday?"

"It smelled like someone in the neighborhood was burning leaves. The air was crisp, but the sun felt really warm. You had messy braids and you were wearing a leopard-print jacket with black fur trim on the cuffs and collar."

I didn't trust my voice, but I remembered my favorite coat quite clearly. I was seven.

He rubbed his face absently while looking into a faraway place that only he could see. "There were four or five of us sitting under the dome monkey bars, and we were talking about what we were going to be when we grew up. Michelle...something—I can't remember her last name—said she wanted to be the president, and Cody Calloway told her he didn't think that girls were allowed to be presidents. Out of nowhere, you exploded on him with this perfect left hook." Foster laughed at the memory. "You just clocked him in the cheek. You stood up with your hands on your hips, and you told him, 'You take that back, Cody Calloway. Girls can be anything they want to be.' Your cheeks were flushed, and you were filled with all this righteous anger." Foster looked at me. "Do you remember that?"

"Yeah," I whispered. My voice... Where was my voice? I cleared my throat. "Of course I remember that. I couldn't go to recess for two weeks because he told on me."

I still didn't know what this was about, but Foster was sort of lost in his hazy memory. He smiled and began again. "I went home that day, and I wrote your name over and over on a piece of paper. I must have written it a hundred times. My mom found the paper a few days later in my sock drawer. She asked me why I'd done that…"

I wanted to know why more than anything I'd ever remembered wanting, but a part of me hoped he'd chicken out.

"I told her I liked the way your name made my heart jump."

Tears welled in my eyes, and I gasped his name. Here I thought his kisses turned my world upside down. I didn't realize his raw heart could unarm me so easily after all the years of building my arsenal of defensive weapons.

Could it be that easy? In all the things I imagined, I never gave myself the room to fantasize about something healthy, a real relationship with him. Why was it that the scariest emotions I'd ever had were the honest ones?

"Foster, I don't know what to say. I don't know what we're supposed to do."

"If we were seven, you would throw me a left hook."

I laughed through tears.

He reached across us to gently wipe the ones that had fallen. "If we were in a movie, the music would swell and we'd rush into a perfect kiss while the credits roll and the camera pans away." His hand fell to his side and his face cemented into the mask of the hardened boy I'd known for four years. "Since it's us, we'll circle like boxers in a ring until one of us

118

remembers the distrust. You'll look at me with eyes full of doubt and wariness, and I'll say something insulting to you so you feel justified."

"Foster..." It was too late. I knew it as soon as he'd dropped his hand.

"You have a piece of lettuce in your teeth. See you tomorrow."

11 CHAPTER ELEVEN

Mr. October

"YOU look worse today than you did when you had two black eyes."

"Why, thank you, Tyler. You always say the sweetest things."

He wasn't wrong. Sleep and I were no longer on speaking terms, because every time I went to sleep, I dreamed The kinds of dreams that woke me up, my heart racing and my skin bathed in cold sweat. I didn't even know what happened in the dreams—I could recollect nothing but the edges of terror that stuck with me long after the lights came back on.

That night, I just didn't bother shutting my eyes.

"You're still having those nightmares, aren't you?"

I nodded and stirred my yogurt aimlessly with no real interest in eating. That was the second thing to go.

"You should talk to someone," Tyler said, his voice lower than normal. Like I was a scared animal he was coaxing into the open.

"I'm pretty sure I'm talking to you. Are you not someone?"

He sighed, and I felt bad. He only wanted to help

me. I knew that. I loved him for caring.

My concern over the state of my health carried over to the state of my brain. The dreams reminded me of my anxiety attack at the roller rink. My head seemed intent on dredging up old memories better left alone, and it wasn't a giant leap to assume it had something to do with the all the guy angst I'd allowed into my life lately.

I'd successfully avoided Foster and Micah for several days. Which also meant I avoided the newsroom, the bathroom, and had skipped two classes. I was phoning in my work and holding my bladder, and I'll admit to being a little put out that neither of the guys seemed to care. But tonight was date night—some demons had to be faced.

The bell rang and Tyler kissed the top of my head and took my barely touched lunch tray for me. On my way to class, I somehow detoured to the other side of campus and found myself staring at the guidance counselor's office door. I hadn't meant to. I would never consciously choose to talk to someone about...me.

But I was there, wasn't I?

A deep breath gave me the fortitude to rap my knuckles on her door, but I chickened out and pivoted to run away and instead ran smack into Ms. Lowell herself.

"Hello, Layney. What a nice surprise."

"Um. Hi." Internal debate: Lie or run? Lie or run?

Ms. Lowell held up a bag of doughnuts. "I'm glad you are here. I couldn't decide between chocolate and jelly, and I know better than to eat both. Come tell me why you're here and I'll split them between us."

I followed her into the office. Lie won, I guess, as

run seemed a touch dramatic by this point.

Ms. Lowell had only been at our school for two years, so she didn't exude that aura of jadedness a lot of the staff developed after years of working in a high school. And she dressed like any minute she was moving to SoHo—an eclectic, funky mix of clothes that I would have loved to be able to pull off, though I lacked the vision.

And part of me loved that she always had a pencil sticking out of her crazy curls. It appealed to me that she felt the need to be prepared to write something at a moment's notice, as I shared that urge but opted to use my pockets for writing instruments.

She cut the doughnuts and chattered at me, not once asking why I wasn't in class. Which was good, since I didn't know. By the time she sat down and delved into her sugar rush, I had formulated a plausible plan.

"Ms. Lowell, I'm doing a story about a sensitive subject, and want to make sure I'm not giving misguided advice or anything."

"Okay," she mumbled through a mouthful of pastry. She pushed the plate of them toward me. "But please eat some of these."

I took the smallest piece, not that I didn't love unhealthy food. I just really wasn't hungry.

"How can I help?"

Ticktock. A cold wave rushed from my head to my toes, and I knew I wasn't ready yet. But she was staring at me with that concerned look, warm feelings emanating at me from across her desk. I suddenly felt just as trapped as I did in my nightmares.

But I really didn't want to live my life this way anymore either. Being afraid of warm feelings—or even feelings in general—was stunting my growth.

"Actually, it's not a story." *Lie or run.* "My friend has a secret. It's a big one. But she won't tell me or anyone about it. Is that going go make her go crazy or something? I mean, if she just pretends it isn't there, can she still have a normal life?"

"Sometimes, talking about our fears can lessen the fear. I can't say she'll never have a normal life, but I think her life would be better without the burden of keeping a big secret all by herself, don't you?"

Easy, Layney. This woman knows all the tricks. "I don't know. I mean, she said it happened to her a long time ago. And that she thought the worst of it was over—she never thinks about it anymore. She'd moved on, totally. But lately, she's been having bad dreams."

Ms. Lowell stopped eating. Elbows on the table, she propped her head on her hands. "When something bad happens to us, especially when we are young, our brains will sometimes protect us from it until we are strong enough to deal with the issue. It's not uncommon for people to completely black out an experience for years and revisit it only when they feel safe enough to face it."

"So, she's strong enough now?" That sucked. The universe seemed pretty unfair. *Glad you're over your trauma, kid. Have some nightmares on the house.* "If she's ready to face it, does she have to, like, talk about it?"

"Repressing is a natural instinct, but it doesn't allow for healing. Coming out of repression can be very similar to reliving the original fear. I'm sure not everyone who needs help gets the help they need, and that may not necessarily mean they won't be okay. But it sure is a lot easier. I'd suggest that you tell your friend to open up to someone. A parent, a friend, and adult she trusts, maybe a professional if she'd feel better telling her secret to someone she doesn't know. But I'd say she is ready to tell someone."

"Why?"

"She told you she had a secret, and she asked for advice. It sounds to me like she knows she can't do this alone and is ready to at least start opening up."

Not so sure about that. "I'll see if I can convince her. You've been a lot of help." I pushed away from the desk and uneaten doughnut.

"Wait." Ms. Lowell pulled out her pad of hall passes and scribbled me a note to get back to class. "Layney, please tell your friend that I would be happy to talk to her at any time if she feels comfortable with me. In fact"—she wrote her number on the back of a business card—"please give her my cell-phone number in case she wants to talk after school hours. Or weekends."

The light of recognition shone in her eyes. She knew. She knew the secret was mine. Of course she knew. Just as I knew taking that card from her outstretched hand meant one more rung into the abyss. But I took it and I nodded. Then I fled.

I thought all day about what she said. Maybe I could just tell one person. But who? I got home at six and found my mother cooking dinner in the kitchen, where she spent the bulk of her time. Mom is a foodie.

I adored my mom, but we were so different. She had wanted children desperately but didn't get pregnant until she was forty-five and Dad was fifty. During the long wait, she baked. A lot. She bakes when she's happy. She bakes when she's sad...worried, frustrated. Her oven is to her what written words are to me.

Despite my long-awaited conception, my folks didn't suffocate me with the over-adoration some people might have succumbed to. They gave me a longer leash than a lot of my peers.

And they went to bed early.

"How was school today?" she asked.

Horrible. "Fine. I have an interview tonight. How was home?"

"It was a good day. Can you set the table, sweetheart?"

I nodded, stopping at the cabinets next to her. "Hey, Mom...I was wondering...um." She looked up from chopping salad veggies, her face so open and sincere.

I just couldn't.

"I was wondering what you want for Christmas."

She rolled her eyes. "Heavens, Layney. Christmas is months away."

"Yeah."

My heart raced and my hands shook while I tried to place the plates gently. This was crazy. She was my mother. She would understand. Logical Layney knew that. Layney Unhinged, however, was apparently in control right then—and very out of control.

I retreated to my room until Mom texted me that dinner was done. My stomach fluttered, and the thought of pot roast churned all the acid into sludge.

Then the doorbell rang.

"Layney," Mom called up the stairs. "There's a boy here to see you."

Thanks for texting me the dinner message but yelling about the boy, Mom.

Boy?

It couldn't be Ty. Mom would have used his name. That meant the boy would be unexpected. Micah or Foster? Which one was it? And if I were honest with myself, which one did I want it to be? I mean, if I couldn't choose neither, of course.

Mom called up again. "Layney, did you hear me?"

"Yeah, Mom. I'll be right down."

I checked my reflection, and the mirror showed me a ghost white girl I didn't recognize. I pinched my cheeks and bit my lip. I saw that in a movie once. I didn't really notice a difference in my face, though.

I was so not ready to deal with either of them. Micah would be the easiest on my oh-so-fragile psyche right now.

I summoned all my thoughts and energy on Micah. His gorgeous blue eyes, the color of the deepest ocean water. The slow, seductive smile that belonged to a man, not a sixteen-year-old boy. The flash of jewelry in his mouth that never failed to make my insides quiver like JELL-O.

I smiled. See? I could do this. I wasn't unable to navigate the waters of my own life after all. I was still the captain of this boat.

Micah treated me well. He asked about things that interested me, knew how he felt about me, and best of all, he never kissed another girl while he was my boyfriend.

But as I pushed myself out of my bedroom and toward the stairs, I realized that it was Foster I wanted to see.

Oh my God. I almost stumbled down the stairs.

Foster. I wanted Foster? Really?

I was pinning my hopes on Beelzebub?

I grabbed the rail to slow myself down. It didn't really matter who I wanted to be waiting in the foyer. Whoever was down there was down there already.

I mustered my courage, tamped down my nervous bile, and held my chin high as I hit neared the bottom.

My mother was making small talk with Alden.

"Frank?"

"Um, hi, Layney." He blushed, but that was nothing new. He always blushed when he had to speak to me.

"I thought you said your name was Alden, dear," Mom said.

"It is, ma'am."

Poor Mom. She frowned and looked at me for an explanation.

"Frank, I mean Alden, what are you doing here?"

"Jimmy asked me to make sure you made it to the date okay. He said sometimes your car doesn't run so good, so my dad is waiting for us outside."

"Your dad is giving me a ride to my date?"

"Us. He's giving us a ride. Jimmy said I needed to stay with you in case something went wrong, like the creepy artist guy."

My heart disengaged from my ribcage and plummeted into my already iffy stomach. Foster sent Alden as my chaperone? Obviously, he no longer cared whether I lived or died. Here I thought I'd been hiding from him—maybe he was avoiding me instead. No wonder it had been so easy.

I pulled out my editor-in-charge voice. I couldn't afford to let Alden witness my disappointment. "Alden, the date isn't until 8:00. Why are you here now?"

"Jimmy said you like to get there early and he told the date to be there at 7:45."

I knew it. All this time, he'd been getting the guys there earlier than me. Asshat. I hated him.

"I'll meet you there, Alden."

"But Jimmy said—"

"I'll meet you there." *Don't scare the poor boy.* "Foster usually stays out of sight, so you'll need to find an out-of-the-way spot. I'll text you if I need help." I guided him to the door. "It will be fine. I feel safer already."

"Really?"

I smiled. "Bye, Alden." I pushed him gently—well, mostly gently—out the door and slumped against it once I'd gotten him through the threshold.

My mother looked at me like I was a lopsided layer cake that needed her attention, but she wasn't sure where to start. "Would you like to borrow my car tonight, sweetie?"

"Yes, please."

The International Language of Love, for what it's worth, is not Czech.

Mr. October, Emil, was a foreign exchange student from Prague. He had really great cheekbones and thick, spiky blond hair. I loved that he blushed when he smiled.

Emil and I stared at each other over the dim sum variety plate between us. The only Chinese restaurant in town used to be a BBQ place. They never changed the decor for some reason. The food was great, but it was always a little disconcerting to eat mu shu pork at a wagon-wheel table. The owners had even left all the

John Wayne memorabilia up, and the bar still served bowls of peanuts.

Emil and I breezed through the pleasantries based on what little English Emil knew. This meant we had forty-five minutes of nonverbal communication to get through.

But Emil was also very friendly and smiled a lot. He refused to take a dumpling first, so I finally broke down and put one on my plate.

He nodded and placed one on his plate but did not eat it.

I stretched for my water glass and he did the same. So I smiled and pushed my plate one inch to the left.

Emil pushed his plate one inch to the right.

I smiled. He smiled.

I couldn't resist the urge, so I scratched the tip of my nose.

You guessed it.

If he hadn't been so earnest about it, I might have thought he was messing with me. The poor guy had only been in the country for two weeks, though. I felt sorrier for him getting stuck with me than the other way around.

"Do you like ice cream, Emil?"

He nodded and his eyes lit up. "Yes. Ice cream is very good."

"Do you like pizza?

"I like pizza. Americans make well of it."

My mind wandered to Ms. Lowell's suggestion that my friend "talk" about her secret. I tried to talk myself out of it, but after a few moments of not talking, I couldn't help myself.

"So you really don't understand anything else I am saying?"

He smiled and nodded.

"I could tell you my deepest, darkest secret, then. And you wouldn't even know, would you?"

He gestured to his plate. "This very good."

"Would it surprise you to know that Foster was right? That I did want him to break up with me even before he went to that party?"

Emil watched my lips closely while I spoke, picking out the words he knew. "Party! Yes, party is fun for me also."

"I wanted him to break up with me because I didn't want him to touch me." I took a deep breath. It didn't help. "I was afraid if he touched me that it would feel ugly. Tainted."

Emil's forehead crinkled as he concentrated. "But ugly is not pretty Layney from newspaper. Layney is pretty, like the flower called rose."

"Thank you." I took a bite of dumpling. My stomach didn't reject it. I took that as a good sign. "I just didn't want him to know. I didn't want anyone to know. I wish I could unknow it myself."

"I am sorry, but my English is not so good. I think you are—how you say?—sad."

I nodded. "Yes, Emil. You are right. I am sad tonight."

"My friend in Prague. When sad I give to her chocolate." He looked out the window and pointed to a convenience store. "We go, yes?"

I nodded. He stood and offered for my hand. At the store, he bought two candy bars, and we walked around the block a couple of times eating chocolate and not talking. Whether or not he got the gist of my one-sided conversation at the restaurant, I didn't know. But he did get the gist of what I needed that night—a friend—and he was willing to give it to me.

12 CHAPTER TWELVE

Mr. November

*I*T *all started when I walked in the room and saw him sitting there. Waiting for me.*

A moll knows when she's been set up.

Frankie was crooning his way through the speakers—they don't make them like Frank anymore. Dino would be next. I'd been here before. Some would call me a regular. A junkie.

My eyes found their target again—and he wasn't alone. The good ones never were, were they? The steam obscured my vision just enough to make him look dangerous. Maybe he was.

I stopped at the counter. "Coffee. Black." I told the barman. I was going to need it.

The screech of the espresso machines matched the noise in my head. I fed myself a slug of bitter to brace my nerves for the interview. It went down easy, like a good roast does. Only later would the acid eat me from the inside out. Just then, it slid down the gullet just right.

I joined them at the table. Made the small talk. I won't lie. He made me a little nervous, Mr. November. I'm sure I wasn't the only dame he intimidated. He was the strong, silent type.

Guys like him didn't come along every day. And dames like me, well we were putty in their hands, weren't we? The baby blue eyes, the pouty lips…

The way he hardly looked up from his Nintendo DS, even when sipping on his Vanilla Frappe he'd ordered with no coffee because Mr. November wasn't allowed to have caffeine after eight o'clock at night.

According to his mother.

Who joined us at Java Junkies.

Because my date was only ten-years-old.

I shook myself out of my pulp-fiction daydream. I didn't get to be Philip Marlowe, and JJ Burke was definitely no Lauren Bacall. Everyone on my staff was getting fired tomorrow. And I was strongly contemplating taking up violence to their persons as well.

I got that he was the only Mensa Club member in our school. I even understood that his genius was a novelty worth exploring—being a ten-year-old junior. But he most certainly should not be dating anyone, let alone me. Why his mother signed off on the calendar at all made me wonder about her—especially since she'd been glaring at me since I sat down.

"So, JJ, what game are you playing?" I asked while keeping eye contact with Mommy. Just in case she thought I was putting a move on him. He was cute but really not my type.

"Pokemon."

"Oh." I knew nothing about Pokémon, other than we used to buy the trading cards but never knew what we were supposed to do with them on the playground. I think each of us had about ten cards that we just carried with us and compared at recess. "Is it fun?"

"No. It's horribly boring. It's like a punishment

having to even turn it on. That's why I take it everywhere I go." He looked up long enough to fire off a stunningly sarcastic facial expression at me.

Well, okay then. Reaching, I offered, "Do you have any other hobbies?"

He sighed, exasperated with me already, and shook his head at his mother before he looked at me again. "I find knitting to be quite soothing when I'm not too busy with my schoolwork, early college applications, chess tournaments, and practicing the twelve languages I speak fluently. Not to mention the seven instruments I play." He rolled his eyes. "I don't have time for hobbies." He turned back to his mother. "I see what you mean. Are they all like this?"

Mommy nodded. "I told you. You won't miss out on anything by not dating high school girls."

Wait a minute.

JJ slurped his frappe. "They can't all be this vapid."

"No," she agreed. "Some are much worse."

"Hey!" I wasn't vapid. I was the anti-vapid. I may not have been a genius, but I didn't think I was representative of insipid high school drama queens. Anger coursed through my veins and the roots of my hair itched.

Mommy patted darling, baby boy's head while she answered me. "It's not you, dear. It's just your age group."

Gee, that made me feel better. Not.

She went on, oblivious that her tact-lacking diatribe was causing me distress. "It's just that JJ has been voicing some concerns that he would be missing some of the social elements of the high school experience by skipping through secondary school and on to college this young. This opportunity, to go on a date with a real high school"—she paused. The bitch paused—"girl...has given him much-needed insight."

I looked around for Foster. This had his name all over it. But it was Alden I spied lurking in the corner. Foster seemed to have gone off me completely.

Dennis the Menace tsk-tsked at me. "I can't imagine wanting to spend time with her even when I'm seventeen. As usual, Mother, you were right."

Oh, kicking him would have felt really good. The little punk. "If you were seventeen, you would be all over wanting to spend time with me, pipsqueak."

"Really?" He narrowed his eyes. "Is that why you don't have a boyfriend and are reduced to dating by appointments your newspaper staff makes for you?"

Don't pinch the little boy, Layney. "Okay. Maybe I am a bad example. But I am sure that you will want to date girls your age when you are my age." *Ankle biter.*

"I really don't think so, Layney. My son has always been mature for his age—too mature sometimes. But I can't see him wanting to waste the time with high school crushes." She finished her tea.

Indignant, I addressed her, "Mrs. Burke, if I may, of course he's going to miss out on the high school experience. You can't just expect that his hormones will take a back seat to his intellect when he's my age. He's going to want to go out with girls his own age at some point. Dating in high school doesn't have to be a curse. It can be a lot of fun. If you're not ten, of course." I took a breath. "And for God's sake, JJ, stop slurping your drink. It's driving me nuts."

He slurped even louder. "Mother is correct. High school dating is a waste of my time and energy."

"It is not. You learn a lot by taking chances on other people. It's not like you are going to marry anybody you date—but it's part of growing up."

I frowned. Oh man. This was brutal. Hell was freezing over. Pigs were flying. I was changing my mind. So much for avoiding warm spots in the water.

I kept talking. "You'll be really sorry." I pulled in a long breath. "You'll be really sorry if you try to bypass all the detours." The familiar taste of regret filled my mouth. "You don't want to get to your destination and not remember anything about the trip."

13 CHAPTER THIRTEEN

Mr. December

A WEEK had gone by since I kissed Foster in the hall. We hadn't been alone together since, and that was all right by me. I needed time to marinate in the confusion he was causing.

I'd hurt Foster probably just as much as he'd hurt me. Granted, I didn't kiss anyone at Lauren Parker's birthday party, but I never gave him the chance to explain or make it up to me. I still might have broken things off with him, had I been myself that weekend. But I'd never know, because I hadn't been myself since.

I had work to do, from the inside out. The first step was going to have to be talking to somebody, and that was still going to be the hardest thing I'd yet to do. Unfortunately, my confidence always petered out when I most wanted to use it. I'd tried three more times to get my mother's Christmas list. She responded by baking more potato rolls than one family could eat in five years.

Tyler took the bench in front of me at lunch. "You are deep in thought. Again. Another crisis at the paper, or have you been slipping the tongue to

Lucifer again?"

"Ha-ha. Can I borrow some lip gloss?"

"That's it. I am never helping you with anything girly again."

He would. We both knew it.

He began peeling his orange but stopped when he realized I was staring at him. "What?"

"I used to be more normal."

"Riiiight."

"I'm serious."

He set his orange down. "Okay."

"Something changed." This wasn't going to work. I could tell. My tongue swelled up in my mouth and I couldn't swallow.

"What changed?"

He knew enough that I should just be able to spew the rest out. I mean, Tyler knew about my panic attack, he knew I was trying to talk to my mother because the guidance counselor suggested it, and he knew that everything changed in eighth grade. He was my best friend, and he wanted to help me. An admission from me would most likely not be a surprise in any way. He was just waiting for me to say the words out loud.

The words I just couldn't.

"It's just that Foster cheated on me, so I changed. I have to go."

I bolted out of my seat and ran away before he could even get the word "wait" out of his mouth.

The next day was date night. My last. I was equally relieved and nervous. I imagined it would be some sort of finale and one final humiliation if Foster had his way. He was probably dead-set on a power play to reverse our positions again.

And there was one more thing I had to do. Besides signing up for a psychologist, I mean.

"Well, this is a surprise."

I handed Micah a coffee.

He leaned down and whispered, "Thank you."

The physical sensation played over my nerves. *Skitter, skitter, skitter,* said my synapses. "I owed you one."

He raised his eyebrows. "If that's all it takes to find you waiting at my locker in the morning, I am bringing you a mocha every day."

My gaze found the floor quickly. I sensed him flinch, and he put a little more distance between us.

"Tonight is the last date." I took a deep breath. "And I decided I'm not going to date anyone else for a while."

"I see." His voice was curt. Clipped.

"Do you?" I forced my gaze to meet his. "I'm not sure that you do."

"Look, if you're about to give me one of those 'it's not you, it's me' phrases, do us both a favor and keep it to yourself."

I moved out of the way so he could open his locker. I started to say, "But—" when he stopped me with a frosty look.

Everything I wanted to say was trite. Nobody wants to hear about staying friends or how nice he is. So I opted to tell him all the things he likely had every right to say to me. I rambled. "I'm an idiot. I know I'm throwing something really great away. You can do so much better than me, and I'm lucky you even gave me the time of day. You're probably the hottest guy

I've ever seen up close, and you'd be one hundred times better to me than any other guy in this school."

He slammed his locker. "You're right."

His face was just—he could really turn on the A/C. "It's not like you led me on—you were always the first person to tell me what a flake you are. I guess you were right."

I hadn't led him on. But I hadn't cut him off even when I knew I should have. I had no business inviting other people's emotions into my life when I had no idea what to do with my own.

"Can we just talk? Maybe later?" I asked.

"I don't have a lot to say to you right now."

What he wasn't saying sure was stabbing my heart with a pickle fork, though.

"I don't want you to hate me."

He shrugged. Like I was wasting my time. He started walking away but stopped and faced me again. "I don't want to hate you, but I don't want to like you anymore, either."

I nodded. I knew exactly how that felt, actually.

"It really isn't you, Micah." Hot tears formed in the corners of my eyes. I wished so hard to be another girl at that moment.

He swallowed hard, and the action contrasted with the hard look he'd been trying give me. "Cut me a break, will ya? This is the part where I have to walk away feeling all superior."

I needed to allow him his dignity, so I nodded my assent and let him get stone cold on me again. "I'm really sorry, Micah."

He turned away without another word. I felt so heavy. I wasn't sure how I was going to make my feet move. As I turned, I noticed Foster watching me from down the hall. He actually looked compassionate—which was more than I could deal with right then, so I turned the other way. Making sure to leave plenty of distance from Micah.

***

So, the last place I expected to find myself was climbing a fire escape of Building E on the high school campus at eight o'clock in the evening.

But there I was. My last date. Relief mixed with the anxiety, but neither cancelled the other out completely. The pink heart only gave me the time and place, as usual. I wasn't afraid of heights, but I found the wind a bit disconcerting. And the fear of the unexpected—well, I had that one wrapped in a red bow.

I reached the top rung and slung my messenger back onto the roof. I peered over the ledge cautiously. There was a table set for two, covered in a white tablecloth and set with two silver domed plates, candles, and crystal stemware.

Before I could really process the implications of such a romantic setting, Foster put out his hand and helped me all the way over. "The building is unlocked. You could have just used the stairs."

I brushed myself off. I don't know why. It just seemed like one of those things you do when you complete a difficult physical task. "That would have been one of those things you might have mentioned in the—" I was struck dumb. "Oh my God, are you wearing a tux? Foster, why are you wearing a tuxedo?"

He looked amazing. Like, I'd have volunteered to be a Bond girl to his 007, and that is just all kinds of sick and wrong.

He held his arms out and twirled for my perusal. "I look damn good in a tux."

"So do movie ushers. Why are you dressed up?"

He gestured toward the table. "May I seat you, madam?"

Oh, this was just creepy.

He shuffled me toward the table, pulled out my chair, and called me 'madam' again. After pushing my seat in, he poured a glass of sparkling cider.

I really didn't like the idea of Foster waiting on my date and me like he was some kind of maître d'.

"What is all this?"

"The last one should be special, don't you think? More memorable than all the rest?"

"I don't think I'll forget the dates anytime soon. Plus, I already have a commemorative mug."

Foster rounded the table and took the other seat.

"What are...? No way."

He poured himself a flute of sparkling juice too. "It was either me or Elden. We couldn't feature all the clubs in school and leave out journalism."

"Is *Alden* still my chaperone?"

He shook his head. "Just you and me tonight." Belatedly, he asked, "Is that okay?" The look on his face reminded me of the guileless seven-year-old he talked about last week.

I shrugged. "My soul is probably in mortal danger, but whatever."

"I know." He removed the dome from my plate. "But I brought you food, so how mad are you really going to get?"

"Did you just say 'I know'?"

"And then I offered you sustenance. I'm a really nice guy, right?"

Well, the lasagna looked good. It probably tasted good too, but I just pushed it around my plate for a few minutes while we enjoyed an awkward silence.

"I'm sorry that I gave you a hard time about dating Micah. You were right. It isn't any of my business. He seems like a nice guy." Foster spoke so quietly, I wasn't sure if I imagined his voice or not.

"He is a nice guy. I'm not dating Micah. But you already know that because you saw us in the hall today."

He shrugged. "I suspected."

Our eyes met each other and it felt like I was standing in a patch of sunlight at night. His words were often harsh, but...

Layney Logan, there are two things in this world you don't need to question. One is gravity. The other is Layney Logan.

I didn't know what to do with his words that day. But I think I knew now.

Of course, it had to be Foster. My comic attempts to unburden myself this week should have led me to this moment much sooner, but it was no secret that I was stubborn.

The way he always checked my phone to make sure it was working, hiding in the shadows in case I needed backup, pushing Dean away from me when I felt threatened, the way he kissed me like I was the last thing he wanted but everything he needed.

I haven't been able to get you out of my system in ten years.

My heart raced with the realization of what I was about to do. I planned to emotionally fillet myself, and the rightness of it was as frightening as the act itself.

I closed my eyes to begin, or else...I wouldn't have. Words. They were just words. They couldn't hurt me anymore.

"Foster, I was raped." Okay, I supposed I could have used a smoother segue.

He didn't reply. I suppose I didn't really want him to, not yet.

"I've never said those words out loud to anyone. I don't think I've even let myself think those words." I opened my eyes. I guess I'd emotionally filleted him too by the looks of his face. "It was always more like 'something bad happened,' even in my head. But it was more than something bad. I was raped."

Foster looked like someone just put him on a stage in the middle of the play whose script he'd never seen. He loosened his tie. "I had no idea. I'm sorry. Really, really sorry." I could read his thoughts like he had a teleprompter on his forehead. He looked at the romantic table between us and felt guilty, as if he'd done exactly the wrong thing. "Oh God. The dates… You must fucking hate me. I swear I didn't know."

"No, I don't hate you. It's okay. It happened a long time ago, really. The dates were fine."

His gaze intensified. Another thought across his teleprompter. "How long?"

I shook my head. "A long time—"

"Shit." He pushed back from the table, guilt etching ugly lines into his handsome features. "Layney, when?" But he knew.

I hadn't meant to shatter him, but it was clear I was breaking his heart all over again. "Eighth grade."

I might as well have punched him in the gut.

He stalked to the ledge. I didn't know if I should let him go or follow him. He leaned against the concrete like it was the only thing holding him upright. Then he punched it.

"Foster!"

He held his injured hand close to his chest and collapsed onto the ground, sitting with his back against the ledge. I grabbed the towel wrapped around the bottle of juice and ran to him.

"I'm sorry. I'm so sorry," he told me.

"Let me see your hand."

He shook his head. "I'm fine. I'm being a total jerk. This isn't about me. I suck."

"It's okay. Let me see your hand."

I sat on the ground and tended to his scrapes, worried that he'd broken something. The knuckles were already swelling.

"Did they get the guy? The one who hurt you?"

I wrapped the towel around his hand and pulled it into my lap. "He's dead."

"What?"

"He was in an accident a few weeks after it happened."

"So it was somebody you knew? Tell me if you want me to shut up."

"I knew him. He was my cousin."

"Why didn't you tell anyone? I mean, you could have told me. You know that, right?"

I started to say something, but he interrupted. "Smooth, Foster. You probably would have if I hadn't screwed everything up. When you needed me the most, I betrayed you."

Hearing him say it out loud was like somebody finally pulled the sliver out of my heart. It hurt. It hurt like hell, but it had to be done. Because a person can't live her whole life not putting any weight on her heart. I'd protected it for so long, I'd forgotten what it felt like to let it do its job.

I brought his injured hand to my cheek, and the tears spilled. And they felt good.

"We were kids, Foster. Neither one of us was equipped to deal with it. I should have told my mother. I know I should have. I tried. And I think I might have finally been ready to when my aunt called with the news that he'd died. It wouldn't have done anybody any good by then."

"But you carried that all alone." Foster brought his other hand to my cheek too. "You're so brave."

"No I'm not. I just hid. That's not brave."

"Can you tell me what happened? Do you want to?"

I shuttered my eyes, wanting the shutter out the rest of it too. It seemed too big, too impossible. "We were at Uncle Bob and Aunt Kate's for the weekly Friday card games. We always stayed over on account of all the gin and tonics. Anyway, my cousin, Robbie, was in high school and too cool to hang out with the 'rents, so it was just me watching movies in the rec room after the adults went to bed. Robbie came home from a party, agitated and strange."

My lungs still worked the air in and out, my heart kept its beat, but I floated outside of my body and watched from above, going back and forth to the roof and basement family room. Safe and apart from both girls.

"Robbie wanted me to have a drink with him. He still had some of his fifth and didn't want to waste his buzz. I didn't want to, but he said…he said…" This was getting harder instead of easier. I steeled my nerves, detaching a little more. "He said I would be safe. That I could trust him. He told me that I should find out how I handled my alcohol someplace where I wasn't in danger of getting out of control."

I could smell the booze and remembered the sickly sweetness of the cola coupled with the hot bite of the whiskey. I wanted to retch. Foster held me close, stroking my hair and encouraging me to keep talking.

"I don't remember much more."

"One drink?" he asked.

I shook my head. The unbearable part was coming. The unthinkable. "I didn't even finish it."

The solidness of Foster tightened around me. "Your cousin roofied you?"

I didn't answer—I couldn't. It was too horrible to imagine. What kind of person did that? Who would offer a young girl safety and use her trust to degrade her?

Foster's breath came out in harsh barks, and I realized he was crying. Or trying not to.

"The next day, he apologized. He said he was just out-of-his-mind drunk. That he couldn't believe he did that to me. I don't think he was ever sober again after that. My aunt kept calling my mom. She was so worried about him. He kept disappearing and was high all the time. She was afraid he was killing himself—I think maybe he was."

"I wish I could kill him."

I pulled back to look at Foster. "I'm sorry that I couldn't trust you then. I was so confused. I felt so dirty, Foster. I was afraid you would feel it all over me if you touched me."

"I was confused too, you know. And I don't know if I will ever feel right again knowing how much I hurt you when you needed me the most." He wiped my tears with his thumb. "When we kissed...did I...did you?"

147

"No," I reassured him. "I have a lot going on in my head—but kissing you never made it worse. I promise."

Some of the tension left his body. "I suppose if I start acting nicer to you, it's going to piss you off."

I stroked his face, wiping away his tears too. "I want you to treat me normal, please. Except—" I looked so deeply into his eyes it felt like I could see his soul. He wanted to be there for me. He wanted me. "I need a time-out from the kissing. There are some things I need to deal with. I'm not ready for more than friendship right now."

"Sure. I understand. Do you think it's too late for us?"

I knew the answer he was hoping for, but I couldn't give it to him. "I don't know, Foster. I'm not in a place where I can conceive of life with or without you. I just don't know."

"Whatever you need, I'm here."

I nodded. "If I figure out what that is, you'll be the first to know."

14 CHAPTER FOURTEEN

ACROSS the table, Foster rubbed his temples and pointed to my Excedrin bottle. I tossed it to him, and he popped two without water and surveyed the scene in front of him.

We'd lost control again. Everyone was talking at once, Mr. Blake was listening to Jimi Hendrix on his iPod, and Alden and Evie were really arguing with each other. Something I'd noticed them doing more and more of. I gestured to them with my eyes, and Foster smirked.

I stood and cleared my throat. Several times. I shot Foster *the look*, so he whistled. And then winced from his headache.

"The floor is yours, Ms. Logan."

"Thank you, Mr. Foster." I held up the calendar. "Hot off the press, gang. Our fundraiser is back from the printer and it looks fabulous." I passed a couple down each side of the table.

"Is your Dates of Doom story ready for this week's issue, Logan?"

I gulped. "Yeah." We were going to send out the paper on Friday and announce the fundraiser sale. "I'll go over it with you after the staff meeting, okay?"

"Ms. Logan, if you want to get me in a room

alone, you don't have to manufacture reasons. Just ask."

I rolled my eyes.

And my heart did this little flutter thing that happened every time he made suggestive comments now.

"Mr. Foster, if I ever get you in a room without witnesses, you might think of running." I made the scissors motion with my fingers. To the rest of the staff, I asked, "How are we doing with the cell phone regulation story?"

"I've got a lead on a planned parent protest," said Maryanne.

Foster perked up. "Spill."

"Josie Carter's mom is organizing a parent call-in day. They are staggering the calls, but essentially, a bunch of parents and relatives are going to call the office on the same day and give them messages for their students—things they would have been able to tell the kids if they still had their cell phones. They want to show the administration that the phones have become an integral part of family communication these days."

"Good work, Maryanne. You plan on covering this one, don't you?"

She beamed at the praise. "I'd love to."

Foster stood up. He was wearing his Charlie Brown shirt again. How was it that such a stupid shirt was suddenly so adorable to me? It was like I was becoming a girl or something.

"I'm guessing we need to keep this as quiet as we can, or they won't be able to pull it off. So nobody discusses the call-in away from this table, got it?" Everyone nodded. I'll admit I liked watching him be a leader. It didn't seem like it was a personal attack on me anymore. "Maryanne, if you need help covering this, let Logan or me know. We'll get you what you need. This is a big story, but I want you to run with it."

She blushed and stammered something unintelligible. I collected the calendars while Chelsea led a brainstorming session about possible features for the next issue. It seemed, for all intents and purposes, like things were coming together.

It had been two months since the night I said the word "rape." I wasn't sure I had done the right thing until the next morning. I rolled over and realized I had slept the whole night through. And while I hadn't relished the thought of facing Foster again in the light of day, I wasn't petrified of running into him either. I felt as if I was poking one foot out of the blanket that had been oppressing me lately. I still had some work to do, but one foot was free.

Foster joined me at a table full of calendar boxes and straightened a pile of papers that didn't need straightening. "So, how are you?"

I opened up a calendar to pretend that I was looking at it. "I'm doing okay. Really."

"I wanted to tell you...I went to a support meeting two weeks ago. For friends and family of people who have been...you know."

He knocked the wind out of me. "What?"

"I probably won't go back...but I went. Just to see if it would help me be normal again. I'm never sure how to act anymore. I don't want to freak you out by being too nice, but I'm afraid that bra-stuffing jokes are crossing the line."

It happened to him too. I didn't really believe that

when my therapist—and, yes I have one now—told me that. Steve told me that Foster's life changed that awful night too.

It didn't sink in—even after he hit the concrete with his fist. But standing with him in a noisy newsroom while he talked about going to a partner-support group made it hit home. He lost his best friend, he carried a lot of guilt, and by the way I caught him looking at me from time to time, he was still in love with me.

Maybe.

"I have a therapist now. I see him once a week." I pivoted away from him slightly to lessen the intimacy, a small protection I still allowed myself. "Maybe sometime you could come with me. If you want. You don't have to or anything. It's probably a dumb idea, right?"

"What would I have to do?" he asked. He was now facing the rest of the room while I still faced the wall. It seemed to be one of those conversations that went better with no eye contact.

"Um. Talk. If you felt like it. Sometimes he just asks me questions."

"Do you talk about me?"

"Sometimes."

"Are you going to tell me what you say?"

"Maybe someday."

"Would you feel weird if I came?"

"Yes. But I would still want you to. If you want, I mean."

He stuffed his hands in his pockets. "Are you glad you're talking to him? Does it make everything…better?"

For the most part, I really liked Steve the

Therapist. Every once in a while, he got on my nerves with all his let's-hug-it-outness. If I got paid a dime every time he said the word "communication," my sixty minutes in the chair would be free. But he was helping me open up.

"I wasn't sold on the idea at first. But I went with my mom twice, and the rest I've been to solo. It's nice to know that, relatively speaking, I'm normal. There's no right way or wrong way to be…afterward. Some girls get overly emo, but some are like me and close off. Steve, my therapist, doesn't talk much about the night it happened. We've been sticking to forward motion progress." I stole a sidelong glance. "Learning to trust, that kind of thing."

I tentatively placed my hand on his shoulder. I'd been told it was up to me when I was ready to pursue more than platonic relationships. Steve said if everyone waited until they were completely healed, nobody would ever date again—even people who had never been sexually assaulted—and that there were degrees of intimacy that I could allow into my life when I felt I was ready for them. It wasn't like I was raped last month—I'd had a lot of time to move forward. But I should expect that sometimes I would regress, and sometimes I would progress.

"Foster, I need to go work on my story some more. Can you handle the rest of the meeting alone?"

"I thought you said it was done."

"Didn't anyone ever tell you women were fickle creatures? It'll be done before deadline. Don't worry."

He rubbed his temples, and I knew the minute I was out the door he would cut the meeting short. But that was okay too. We had so much more leeway with the paper now that we were digital. I still wanted the new software and hoped the calendar would pay for it, but if we kept it the way it was, we'd be fine too.

Once again, I was reminded why I wrote words and didn't play sports. I had a terrible arm and every rock I threw missed the window. Some of them didn't even hit the house.

Frustrated, I kicked a rock hard enough to stub my toe. I started hopping and chanting, "Shit, shit, shit." Why was my life such a farce?

"Is there a particular reason you are doing the bunny hop in my front yard, Logan? Is this a complicated hex ritual or something?"

I turned around slowly, on one foot, and faced a very wry Foster. "Yes, it was a spell to turn you into more of a toad then you already are. Alas, you ruined the whole thing by coming upon me unannounced. Now I'll have to wait until the next new moon."

"It's a good thing you can't aim."

"Why?"

"Because that isn't my window anymore. My little brother and I switched rooms two years ago."

"Oh."

"Now would be a great time to tell me why you are here."

"Oh. Oh yeah. I wanted to see you."

He held out his arms and turned in a circle. "I gathered that much, Ms. Logan. The question remains—why?"

"What are you doing out here anyway?"

"This is my house."

"Why aren't you in it?"

"I went for a walk. I saw your car on the corner

and figured you broke down, so I came back. Why are you here?"

This really wasn't going the way I planned it in my head. "Well, I thought we could go for a walk. To the swings."

"She wants to go to the swings," he said to no one in particular. "You're a very unusual girl."

"Thank you." I sent him a cheery smile. "That is the best compliment I've had in years."

We meandered through the deserted streets to the park a couple of blocks from his house. We took our spots on the swings where we used talk for hours. I don't remember ever actually swinging on them, but we would twist them toward each other sometimes for a stolen kiss now and then.

"I finished my piece about what the teenage girl wants."

"Well, I'm so glad you didn't just email it to me or wait until morning like a sensible person."

I pulled the story out of the side pocket of my jacket. "I wanted you to read it on paper."

"How very old-school of you." He raised his chin to look at the sky. "It's kind of dark here. If you hadn't noticed."

I pulled a flashlight out of a different pocket.

"You never told me you were a Boy Scout," he quipped. "Why am I suddenly nervous to read this?"

I shrugged.

"'What a Girl Wants' by Layney Logan," he read aloud and proceeded to read the rest that way too:

When the question is first asked, it seems like a no-brainer. They want a great boyfriend. What girls are looking for when it comes to the perfect boyfriend, though, that is much tougher. And is there such a thing?

Being sent on an assignment is always a rush. I've dived from cliffs with Olympiads, spent a day at boot camp with the Navy recruiters, and eaten some pretty interesting dishes from the High School Skill Center kitchens. None of these, not even the calamari prepared by the freshman culinary class, struck terror into my heart like the prospect of going on twelve blind dates.

I wasn't much of a dater, which is why I got the story pitched to me. Who better to solve the puzzle than someone looking at it from the outside?

So I set upon the task of finding that elusive something that some guys have and other guys wish they had. What I found was impressive. Some high school boys define themselves by their peers, some by their dreams, and some by their wallets. They are characterized by their family ties, their sense of humor, their cultivated skills, and their natural talent. Some want a girl for a week. Some hope it lasts a lifetime. Some don't even want a girl at all.

After each date, I made copious notes about what made that boy more attractive. Was it his confidence? His compassion? Did he have great hair, piercing eyes, a sense of style all his own? Maybe he was willing to be a friend first.

Maybe he had some not so shining characteristics.

Some guys think it's all about them—what they want. Some guys have a scary way of idealizing the girls they consider to be the epitome of the female form. Some wish to skip their adolescence altogether.

I realized quickly that the more notes I made, the

more confused the issue became. Maybe that is where chemistry comes in. Maybe you can't put that on paper.

Maybe what a girl wants couldn't be defined by twelve blind dates and a jaded reporter.

An apology to all the hopeful young men who opened this article and thought they'd finally be handed the answer to their quest for the Holy Grail. I'm no closer to knowing what girls want then when I started—and believe me, I've been thinking of little else for a several months.

My best advice is to be yourself. Unless you're psychotic, then you might want to try a different tactic.

Some girls will love you for your intelligence, your spirit, or your smile. Some girls will fall all over themselves if you even make the smallest effort to understand them. Some girls don't care how you act as long as you drive a nice car. (And some boys deserve those kinds of girls. I'm just sayin'.)

Some girls will require a lot more from you than most guys are willing to give. This is the girl you'll need a lot of patience for, because she will lead you down blind paths and up steep hills. The challenge will be staying true to who you are while pursuing this person.

She'll wring you out, simultaneously repel and attract you, and question your every intention. She'll be the biggest pain in the asphalt you've ever had.

She'll need you to understand what she won't tell you, believe in her when she extends no faith in you, and not give in to her when she wants to roll over you. She'll expect that you'll always be there, even when she avoids you. She'll want lots of

157

independence but want you to need her desperately. She'll expect you to be smart but treat her like she's smarter than you.

Hopefully, you'll believe she's worth it in the end.

So, it is with my deepest regrets that I cannot solve the mysteries of the universe. I don't know what girls want anymore than I understand why I've seen adults doing the Soulja Boy dance at wedding receptions. Some things are just meant to stay mysteries.

While I can't explain what all girls are looking for when it comes to boys, I can tell you they'll know it when it makes their heart jump. As for this girl, I think I've finally figured it out.

Foster stopped reading and looked up before he turned the page. I think I was dazzling him, but I'm not sure.

"Go on." I nodded toward the paper. "Turn it."

Slowly, he flipped the page…

Jimmy Foster
Jimmy Foster
Jimmy Foster
Jimmy Foster
Jimmy Foster
Jimmy Foster
Jimmy Foster
Jimmy Foster… (one hundred times)

ABOUT THE AUTHOR

Gwen Hayes lives in the Pacific Northwest with her real life hero, her children, and the pets that own them all. She writes romantic fiction for teens and adult. She is represented by Jessica Sinsheimer. For more information about Gwen, please visit her website at
www.gwenhayes.com

CPSIA information can be obtained
at www.ICGtesting.com
Printed in the USA
LVHW041801040820
662390LV00004B/621

9 781492 981671